CRIPPLE
WOLF

JEFF BURK

ERASERHEAD PRESS
PORTLAND, OREGON

ERASERHEAD PRESS
205 NE BRYANT
PORTLAND, OR 97211

WWW.ERASERHEADPRESS.COM

ISBN: 1-936383-86-1

Some people say that writing is a solitary and lonely profession. Those people are full of shit.

Special shout outs to:
Rose O'Keefe, Carlton Mellick III, Boing Boing, Cameron Pierce, Chrissy Horchheimer, Samuel, Deats, Topless Robot, Whitney Streed, Rachel E. Graves, Troy Chambers, Jeremy Robert Johnson, Alan M. Clark, Wizard Magazine (R.I.P.), The World Horror Convention, John Skipp, Ryan Harding, Mykle Hansen, Brian Keene, Norwescon, Batman, Powell's Books, Wil Weaton, Edward Lee, Kevin Shamel, Andrew Goldfarb, Nate Southard, Wrath James White, Lloyd Kaufman, James Beach, Garrett Cook, PFFR, Bryan Smith, Kevin L. Donihe, Happy Cat, Dave Brockie, RadCon, everyone that makes the yearly trek out to BizarroCon, to the awesome bartenders at Lucky Lab, Ground Kontrol, Bailey's Tap Room, and The Lovecraft Bar, and to anyone else my drug-addled mind is forgetting.

Fuck off to:
You know who you are.

Books by Jeff Burk

Shatnerquake
Super Giant Monster Time!
Cripple Wolf (stories)
Pothead
Homobomb
The Slaughterhouse Thrills
Shatnerquest
Lord of the LARPers
Dinosaurs Attack
Oh Shit! We's Gonna Cut You!
Hipster Hunter
Pirate Cat
Shatnerpocalypse

CONTENTS

1
NIGHTMARE AT 40,000 FEET

He didn't really want to kill the baby but he did it anyway.

He snatched the infant out of its mother's arms and sunk his teeth into the baby's soft chest. It squealed like a stuck piglet.

The mother's screams pierced his ears. He bitch-slapped her with his hairy paw but she kept screaming, staring at her mutilated baby dangling from his other claw. He swiped at her again and, at that exact same moment, the plane hit a rough patch of turbulence. His claw sliced cleanly through her neck and the rocking of the cabin sent the head bounding into the overhead storage compartment and straight off into the middle of a row of passengers.

Panic exploded in the crowd.

He snorted, his senses aroused by the blood, sweat, and fear in the recycled air. The infant convulsed in his claws. He lapped its blood with his wide flat tongue and then tossed the little pork chop aside.

He spun and wheeled toward his next victim.

"Now boarding Fetish Flights #33 to Portland, Oregon, United States."

The nurse pushed Benjamin Kurtz in his wheelchair to the end of the line. Well, she wasn't really a nurse. Her plastic form-fitting uniform and thigh high boots gave that away. But Benjamin had paid her good money to take care of his *every* need during his stay in Tokyo, and getting to the airport was one of his needs. He shifted in his chair, wishing he had to take a shit so she could clean him off one more time before he left.

Benjamin served four tours of duty in Vietnam. On the first, a stray piece of shrapnel ricocheted off his helmet. Nothing but a miracle could explain how he had sustained no physical damage. But after that, his memory was never the same.

On his fourth tour, while on patrol, he was attacked by a wolf. The attack put him in the chair and there was something else important but he didn't remember. He spent a while in the infirmary, dead from the waist down, and that's where he developed his diaper fetish. Having those young nurses, still fresh from medical school, wipe the shit from his ass excited him in ways he never before dreamed.

When he was returned to the States, Uncle Sam no longer having use for a crippled soldier, he found out he had a wife. He had just plain forgotten. She had moved on with her life and remarried and, after a few months, he had completely forgotten about her again.

The diaper fetish stayed.

Disability took good care of him and he saved up so, once a year, he could take a vacation to Japan. In the States he occasionally got lucky with a cute pre-med, but most of his nurses were old, fat, hags. In Tokyo, there were establishments that catered to his specific needs.

That's where he met . . . well, he didn't remember her name anymore. Her name didn't matter, what mattered was how she filled out that uniform.

Benjamin eyed the other passengers waiting in line. Near the front was a guy with a bright blond bihawk chatting up a young girl with purple hair. Behind them were two more punks talking amongst themselves. There was a guy who looked like a body-builder, a Japanese Elvis, hippies, and even two fools dressed like clowns.

The normal clientele for Fetish Flights.

The line moved forward and Benjamin took notice of the man directly in front of him. He was wearing a long brown trench coat that was at least two-sizes too large and an oversized brown fedora pulled down to hide his head. In the crack between his coat and hat, it looked like his neck was covered in purple spandex. When he stepped forward, in-between his jacket and boots, Benjamin could see the man was wearing purple tights. *He looks like a real pervert.*

10

Soon, Benjamin was at the front of the line. The ticket taker was a knock-out blonde wearing a fetish outfit made of strips of black leather connected by metal rings.

"Welcome to Fetish Flights," she said taking his ticket, "enjoy your flight."

"I'm sure I will," he said, staring at her nipples poking through the leather. "But I do need some . . . special assistance."

That's what made Fetish Flights, Fetish Flights. Their staff catered to anyone's desire; the men were Adonises, the women Aphrodites. All were dressed in the finest, and most revealing, fashion of the discerning fetishist.

She glanced down at his ticket. "Of course. We'll have a stewardess attend to you momentarily."

She pushed a button at her station and an even bustier brunette wearing even less came up to Benjamin. His nurse left and the brunette pushed him down the ramp onto the plane. She wheeled him to his handicap seat, which was right next to the boarding door. Next to him was a young, wholesome looking woman holding a very small baby. He grimaced at her. Sometimes people accidentally ended up on Fetish Flights due to their extremely discounted fares.

"Don't worry, he's a heavy sleeper," she said when she noticed Benjamin looking at the child. "He won't be one of those screamers on the plane."

She rocked the baby and said, "It's a full moon tonight. I hope we can see it from the air, it should be beautiful."

Benjamin nodded. A full moon. That seemed important. But he couldn't remember why.

Abdul Omar, otherwise known as Lawrence Talbot on his passport, stared at himself in the mirror of the tiny airplane bathroom. Some days he found it hard to believe it was himself staring back. His hair was two inches long and rather stylishly spiked. He rubbed his smooth chin and remembered a time when there was a bushy beard there. He smirked at himself. With his The Clash t-shirt and blue jeans, he looked just like one of them.

All a part of deep cover.

He pushed a button on his shoulder, so subtle and hidden that only he knew its location, and his forearms popped open revealing two hollowed out compartments perfect for smuggling.

From his left arm he removed a switchblade. He snapped open the weapon admiring its six inch blade. He snapped it shut and slid it into his front pocket.

Abdul took a taser out of his right arm and stuck it into his other pocket.

He snapped shut the compartments and pushed another hidden button on his hip. He lifted his shirt and opened the chamber in his chest. Inside was twelve pounds of C-4 hooked up to a small control panel. He reached in and activated the panel. He knew that when the time came, the explosives would add destructive potential. At the very least, if anyone tried to stop them, he and Mohammad (who was in the next bathroom going through the same preparation) could just take down the whole plane.

Abdul shut his chest and pulled his shirt back down. He smoothed out the picture of Paul Simonon smashing a bass guitar on his shirt and took one last look in the mirror. The clothing, even the bands and logos on them, had been a part of his cover story. To make his story viable he had to immerse himself in this hedonistic culture. He had to watch the TV shows, read the books, and listen to the music. Surprisingly, he found himself enjoying The Clash. The punk group was just randomly selected for him, but the heretic white men actually had some lyrics to which he could relate.

He left the bathroom and walked down the plane's narrow aisles. He stole a quick glance at Mohammad, who was already seated and flipping through an issue of *Wizard* Magazine. As he sat down, he picked back up the cheap paperback he had been reading, *The Conqueror Worms* by Brian Keene. Just some piece of horror dreck and another part of his assigned cover. He read while softly singing under his breath.

"Death or glory. Becomes just another story."

***

Abdul awakened to the roar of over three hundred passengers. *Great Allah, how long was I asleep?* People were standing and screaming and crying. Abdul thought they must already be at the assigned point and Mohammad was making his move.

He sprung to his feet and flipped out his switchblade.

"Everyone! Stay calm and no one will be hurt!"

His voice was not even audible over the chaos in the cabin. He realized that no one was even looking at him. They were all looking at something behind him. Abdul turned around and stared.

A hairy beast was in front of him. Its large paws and arms were wrapped around a man wearing a black latex catsuit while its snout was buried deep in the man's neck. The animal and man were soaked in blood.

The animal's eyes shot up and locked with Abdul's. The thing tossed aside the latex clad corpse and howled like a wolf, its snout dipping down and then straight up in the air. Its thick brown fur was shaggy and matted with gore.

Abdul was frozen. Apart from the fact that he was looking at a monster, there was something else terribly wrong with it. The beast, who was obviously male, was sitting down in the aisle like a human in a chair. Then what he was seeing clicked.

It's in a wheelchair . . .

The creature rolled forward, using its hirsute paws to gain speed. Abdul leapt to the side, throwing himself over vacated seats. He wasn't quick enough. As he jumped, a large paw swiped at him in midair and dug a hole in his stomach just below his hidden chamber. The claw caught hold of his intestines and the creature continued to wheel down the aisle.

Abdul convulsed in shock and couldn't move. He watched his insides unravel and get pulled across the plane. He could just barely turn his head to see the monster run down an old woman in a ball gag and corset. Then his vision went black and white and he could smell roses. Then nothing.

***

Kiichi was nodding his head to the fast beat of the Stance Punks songs playing on his headphones when Kana started to shake him. Kiichi tore off the ear pieces.

"Hey—" he stopped when he heard the screams. Kana stared at him with wide-eyed fear through her hot-pink bangs. Kiichi turned to Yousei, who was already on his feet scanning the cabin.

Kiichi, Kana and Yousei all played in the same punk band, Mouthful of Ants. After three years of playing together, their career took off with their fourth album, *Land of the Rising Scum*. At the record release show they revealed their new live gimmick. Before they went on stage, they all drank a homemade cocktail of fake blood and syrup of ipecac. For the first five songs of their set, all the members of Mouthful of Ants projectile vomited fake blood across the stage, crowd, and each other. That caught the attention of Epitaph Records and then the world. Which placed them onboard the double-deck, wide-body Airbus A380 flying from Tokyo, Japan to Portland, Oregon, U-S-A!

They had dreamed of this moment for years, their first world tour. All that stood between them and their first show on American soil was a thirteen hour and forty-seven minute flight. Well, that and whatever was scaring everyone so much. Kiichi didn't want to die in a plane crash—not before they played New York City.

He stood up to try and see what was happening. It seemed everyone in the passenger area was standing and yelling. The plane held three hundred and twenty-five people in this cabin alone. Kiichi strained his neck but couldn't see what was causing the panic. The three punks were seated in the back of the plane, on the left, next to the windows. Whatever was causing the commotion was happening in the front, to the right.

The girl with the purple hair's body flipped into the air, bounced off the ceiling, and crashed into the middle section of the passengers. People fled toward the back of the plane, climbing over seats and each other to get away from whatever was coming.

"Mega uncool," said Yousei.

The beast tore through the people. It did not pick any specific targets, its claws slashing and slicing through flesh and plush seats alike. The fear-stench of its prey electrified the air. Sometimes it brought some juicy morsels to its mouth, but it wasn't killing for food. It was killing for fun.

People tried to get away but there was just no place to go. A Japanese man dressed as Elvis tried climbing over one of the seats but the creature grabbed his feet and pulled him in close. With a single motion, the beast slashed into the man's gut, sending blood and viscera spraying into the air.

A crusty old man had ignored the fleeing crowd and remained in his seat. His pants were down around his ankles and he was furiously whacking off. A spray of blood from the slaughtered Elvis hit his exposed penis and delivered just the lubricant he was hoping for.

The beast turned to the man and roared in his face, covering him with blood-speckled saliva. The man jerked faster.

The monster grabbed the man's gore-coated cock with one paw and his balding head with the other and tore both off his body in one easy motion. The beast bit into the man's severed face, cracking the skull, and pulled out a snoutful of brains. It threw the penis at a screaming woman and it bounced off her forehead.

"Filthy beast, pick on someone your own size," came a voice from behind the creature.

The cripple wolf turned its hairy maw flinging mucus, slobber, and gore.

Standing in the aisle, between the monster and the rest of its intended victims, a man wearing a purple facemask and a purple spandex bodysuit struck a defiant pose, hands on his hips. On his chest was a shiny yellow "S."

The people behind him cheered. Their savior was here. The one and only, Star Spangler!

15

The monster spun its wheelchair to face the purple challenger. It howled and pushed forward, hard. The Star Spangler ran toward it, drew back his fist, and punched the creature with the force of a Panzer III right on its snout. The last person The Star Spangler hit this hard was the self-proclaimed "indestructible" Destroyo. That blow had knocked the villian's head off his body and through three-blocks-worth of walls before finally coming to a stop in a second grade classroom. The Star Spangler spent time in therapy after that, but he got better.

The hairy thing shook its head, quickly recovering from the resounding blow. Then reached out and sunk its claws deep into the The Star Spangler's forearms. It held the hero firmly in place with his arms outstretched. Blood ran freely from the wounds and began to pool on the floor. The Star Spangler grimaced, trying not to show the pain. The crowd fell quiet.

The beast pulled The Star Spangler's arms further and the cabin filled with the sharp sound of splintering wood. The hero let out a high pitched scream. Then the passengers closest to him began screaming as well. They fell to their knees as blood poured from their ears. His super vocal chords had shattered their ear drums.

With a quick tug, the thing pulled both of The Star Spangler's arms from their sockets. He shrieked as blood from his stumps sprayed across the cabin.

The monster swung the right arm like a club, smacking The Star Spangler across the head. He dropped to his knees and his left arm came slamming down. The Star Spangler crumpled as the beast brought both his shiny purple arms down on top of him again and again.

It roared and tossed the arms aside. Then grabbed its wheels and rolled over the fallen superhero.

Dax Thompson flopped back in his chair.

"Ahhhhh . . ."

The coke surged brain and everything went sharp.

"Whew! Damn Chavez, this is some fine shit."

Chavez took a drag on his joint and adjusted his headpiece. "Told you."

Dax flipped up the tray table and it slid down next to his seat. He leaned forward and looked out over the Pacific Ocean. Chavez and he had been piloting transpacific flights for going on five years. The two got along great, their hedonism providing a quick bond. While their behaviors unnerved some of the flight staff, and would surely terrify the passengers, they had an impeccable record. If anything, all the drugs helped them to focus. Especially when it came to these nearly fourteen hour marathon runs.

Black lights gave the cockpit an eerie glow. In the center of the console, an undulating lava lamp bubbled martian-green in the stoner-light. Bob Marley played over the cockpit's private speaker system.

Dax loved these night runs over open water. On the darkest nights, it felt like he was flying through an abyss. And then the lights of land would begin to twinkle in, like he had just traveled through dimensions.

Or there were nights like tonight. A bright full moon filled the sky, not a cloud obscured the water beneath. The light danced off the black water that seemed to stretch out forever in every direction.

"It's a beautiful night. Times like this, with nothing below and nothing above. Really makes you think," Dax said.

Chavez smirked, "Shit, are you getting into one of your Thoreau moods again?"

"*Chavez! Dax! Are you there?*" Shelly's voice cut in through their headpieces interrupting the reggae. She was one of the stewardesses and she sounded frantic.

Chavez pushed a button on the center console, "Chavez here, what's up?"

It was hard to understand what she was saying. It seemed like there were people screaming in the background. "*...back cabin ... it's killing everyone!*" And then she cut out.

Chavez and Dax exchanged a look.

"I'll call Daryl," said Dax.

The Airbus was a modern marvel of engineering. It

was one of the largest commercial airplanes ever built. The plane had three main passenger compartments—two on the lower deck and one on the upper. The two lower ones were the business class accommodations. The back cabin, where Shelly called from, was the larger of the two and capable of holding three hundred and twenty-five passengers. The front cabin was smaller and held one hundred fifty. The upper deck held two hundred and fifty seats for first class. At full capacity, the plane was capable of transporting seven hundred and twenty-five people, and this night's flight was nearly full.

With such a large number of passengers, the airline staffed the plane with fifteen flight attendants to care for their needs. Five were assigned to the upper deck and the other ten were split into two teams for the business class. Shelly led the back cabin with a staff of seven. Daryl was in charge of the three for the front.

Dax pushed the button for the front cabin, "Daryl, you there?"

"This is Raymond."

"Yo Raymond, what's going on down there? We just got a strange call from Shelly."

"Don't know yet. There's a lot of screaming from the back cabin. Daryl went to check it out."

"Copy, keep us up to date."

"Will do."

Dax flipped off the intercom and the music returned.

He turned to Chavez, "What the fuck you think that's all about?"

The screaming started in the back cabin and did not stop. After two minutes, Daryl decided he should go check it out. He left Raymond in charge. He jogged to the curtains that divided the two compartments, his uniform's chains and metal rings softly clanging. Worried passengers eyed his chiseled frame as he went past. He stopped and listened to the screams and the sounds of fighting. He was pretty sure he could smell blood.

As he grabbed a hold of the curtain, images of terrorists

and slit throats filled his head. He was totally unprepared for what he saw when he pulled it aside.

The cabin looked like a slaughterhouse. Corpses and body parts littered the floors and seats. Blood was splattered everywhere, even on the ceiling.

Most of the surviving passengers cowered at the back of the cabin, huddling together. Others climbed over the seats like they were trying to get away from something.

Daryl scanned the room and saw what was causing the carnage. A large hairy animal of some sort was tearing its way through the people. Limbs, bodies, and gore flying in its wake.

He grabbed the intercom handset on the wall next to him and pushed the button for the cockpit.

"This is Daryl. Get the marshals. We have an animal loose in the back cabin."

Agent Willis came back to his seat and sat down next to his partner. He had just been called to the cockpit over an emergency that was apparently happening in the lower cabins.

"What's going on?" asked Smith. A red foam ball bounced on the end of his nose.

Willis snickered.

"Shut up, man. You don't look any better."

Both agents wore red foam noses, rainbow colored polka-dot jumpsuits, blue over-sized shoes, and white gloves. Their wigs, however, were different. Willis had a neon green mad-scientist hairdo and Smith had a skull-cap with a bright blue frohawk.

Their cover was always assigned before flights. But the agency really fucked it up this time. They were told there was an international clown convention happening in Portland and the Japanese branch of the International Federation of Clown Sciences and Enthusiasts would also be on their flight. But Willis and Smith were the only two clowns on board.

"I'm sorry, I can't help it," answered Willis as he controlled himself. "Seems there's some kind of animal loose in the back cabin."

"An animal? What kind?"

"Don't know. Someone probably just snuck their dog aboard."

"Alright," Smith stood up, "let's take care of this."

Willis followed him and they descended the narrow stairwell to the lower level. Their shoes squeaked with each step.

As soon as they were down, a strong copper smell attacked their nostrils and screams assaulted their ears. They drew their SIG P226s and went to the dividing curtain where a visibly terrified steward was standing and passengers, some with terrible injuries and covered in blood, were running through.

Next to them were two heavily pierced, scantily-clad, punk girls with huge tits. They saw the guns and gasped. One threw herself at the other. "Hold me, I'm scared."

"What's the situation?" asked Smith.

The steward pulled back the curtain and the agents saw the massacre that was the back of the cabin. Both agents held their guns out and went in.

They rushed down the aisle toward the beast mauling a young woman in a metal brassiere. They stopped about ten feet away and each fired a shot into the back of the thing's head. It dropped the woman's body and pivoted to face them.

"Head into the next cabin," Smith yelled and motioned with his head backwards. Some passengers understood and ran down the opposite aisle.

"Are you seeing what I'm seeing?" asked Smith.

Willis turned his attention to the animal; a shaggy, gore-soaked combination of wolf and man, sitting in a wheelchair.

"I think it's crippled," commented Smith.

The beast began wheeling toward them at a speed that would win a gold medal at the Special Olympics.

Both agents opened fire.

In order to be an armed Air Marshall, one must be an expert marksman. Just one stray shot could depressurize an entire airplane. Agents Smith and Willis were the best deadeyes in the business. Every shot they landed should have been a fatal blow but the thing did not even slow down. It slammed into them, wheeled past slashing its claws, and spun around to face them. Both agents now lay on the floor with their polka-dotted legs cut off at the knees. The men helplessly thrashed about while they bled out.

The beast, satisfied at the disposal of this nuisance, spun to see the people running down the opposite aisle toward the next compartment.

It howled and wheeled toward the escape route.

"Oh shit," Daryl said to Raymond as they watched the monster wheel straight at them.

Daryl glanced at the people still trying to get out. There were still a large number coming down the aisles and they were only slowing each other down. He looked back at the monster and knew that it would be upon them soon.

"We have to shut the emergency doors," he said to Raymond.

"But there are still people in there."

"That thing will be here in moments."

Raymond hesitated and then nodded. Both of them went to the sides of the entryways and hit the emergency buttons. As a security measure, the plane had automated steel doors, eight inches thick, which could be activated at a moment's notice. In the event of a hijacking, the doors could isolate the affected area from the rest of the plane.

Passengers continued to rush past and when the doors started to slowly slide over, the crowd surged forward. Daryl and Raymond stood back as people continued to squeeze through. Then the doors shut, cutting off the back cabin.

People begged in both English and Japanese for the door to be opened and then a loud crash resounded and the creature hit the doors. The screaming rose in volume and then fell as the few survivors in the back cabin were scattered away from the steel doors.

Daryl looked over at Raymond who was visibly shaking. The front cabin was now filled with lucky passengers who had escaped the massacre. People were crying and covered in gore. It was hard to tell who was actually hurt and who was just splattered.

"Gather up the other attendants and help anyone who's hurt," he said to Raymond.

He then went over to the intercom and rang up the cockpit.

"Daryl here, I think we got it contained."

Kiichi, Kana, and Yousei reached the doors just as they snapped shut. They were immediately pushed forward by the other passengers attempting to escape. The force of all the bodies pressed them flat against the doors. Hands reached around and banged on the steel and voices pleaded for them to open.

"Scene's turning Dennis Hopper," Yousei strained to be heard over the crowd.

Kana nodded and pointed to their left, the direction they just came from. The three wormed their way through the mass of bodies.

Then the beast attacked from the opposite aisle in a fugue of sharp teeth and claws. People flew into the air as its wheelchair plowed forward. The thing slashed blindly and tore through soft flesh and bone.

The three punks broke into a full run toward the back of the plane.

The rear back cabin had a small hallway that led to four bathrooms and a service/cooking station for the flight attendants.

Kana ran into the cooking station. There was a steel counter with cups built into it containing all the silverware. She grabbed from on the cups and spun around with the weapon held out.

It was a plastic spork.

"Spastic," she shouted and threw the utensil to the floor.

Other passengers had seen the punks flee to the back and they were now seeking shelter in the same area.

Kiichi and Yousei were still at the end of the hallway, right by the seating area, frantically searching the doorframe.

22

Kiichi glanced up and saw the monster was still tearing into people at the opposite end of the back cabin.

"Spicy," Yousei exclaimed as he found the button that activated the panic doors. The steel barrier started to slide across. Right before it closed completely, the beast turned and met Kiichi's eyes from across the cabin. It growled and the door shut tight.

"People, please try to stay calm."

Raymond's voice boomed over the front cabin's public intercom. In the crowd, the flight attendants, along with a few passengers with basic first aid knowledge, worked to provide medical help for those that needed it. The injuries were many and severe. Some needed tourniquets for lost limbs, others were just being made comfortable until they bled to death. People were understandably panicked and control needed to be regained.

"I've been talking to the cockpit."

That got the passengers' attention. The front cabin quieted and, oddly, the smell of blood seemed to grow stronger.

"The animal is contained—"

As if on cue, the monster howled from the other side of the steel doors.

"—and we are closer to Portland than we are to Tokyo, so our only option is to continue on to our destination. The pilots have been in communication with PDX and medical and security help will be waiting for us. We just need to wait this out until we land."

"And how long will that be?" someone in the cabin yelled out.

Raymond paused and composed himself, "Six hours."

2
CURSE OF THE CRIPPLE WOLF

Sister Mishka Holloway picked up the baby while everyone else ran past it. It would have been easy to mistake the child as dead; its chest was split open and on the floor was a small tendril of intestine.

But when she almost stepped down on the body, Sister Mishka noticed that its tiny chest was moving ever so slightly. The poor thing wasn't dead yet. Instinctually, she scooped up the bloody infant and, holding it close to her habit, she ran.

The rest was a blur, but suddenly she found herself locked in the small hallway that led to the bathrooms and kitchen. She sat down and leaned against the wall.

There were six other passengers – the three Japanese punks, a shirtless American man with the physique of Stallone (steroid-infused *RAMBO III* years) flexing at no one in particular to console himself, and a young American hippy couple. It looked like the man's lower ribs had been ripped away. His dreadlocked partner tried to console him through a stream of tears as she held in his guts through blood-stained tie-dye.

Sister Mishka looked down at the child and gagged. Its torso was torn so wide she could see the tiny heart beat and small lungs expand and contract like spongy bellows.

She rocked the baby against her breast and softly hummed "Hey Diddle Diddle" while she waited for it to die.

The Star Spangler opened his eyes and tried to prop himself up. For some reason he couldn't get his arms to work. Then he remembered – they were gone. Fortunately, his healing powers had immediately sealed the wounds and he didn't bleed to death.

With some struggle, he sat up and then got to his feet. He looked around the cabin. Apart from the numerous bodies,

24

it appeared he was alone. Then he heard growling and scratching. He turned and saw the monster attacking a metal door at the back of the cabin.

As if alerted by some sixth sense, the beast immediately turned its head and locked hungry eyes on him.

"Fuck." The Star Spangler turned and ran the other way. He heard the squeak of the monster's wheels as it raced after him.

The front exit was blocked off by another steel door. The Star Spangler kicked it and yelled for someone to open.

He turned his head and saw the beast was right behind him.

"Fuck!" He screamed and roundhouse kicked the creature. The thing immediately grabbed his leg and, effortlessly, wrenched it back. The limb tore away at his waist and The Star Spangler was left balanced on one leg.

"Fuck!" He screamed once more and the monster began to beat him with his severed leg.

Raymond heard the struggle on the other side of the door as the monster claimed another victim. He wanted to help the person out, but opening the door could mean death for everyone else in the front cabin.

The cabin was too noisy for anyone else to have heard the attack. Daryl was organizing a retreat to the upper cabin. The monster was in a wheelchair, so if it got free, he figured it would probably have a problem with the stairs.

Most of the passengers were already on the upper level but some of the extremely injured were too hard to move. Raymond walked across the cabin passing at least two dozen people missing limbs or trying to hold in their guts. Attendants and some passengers assisted the wounded as best they could, but the plane just wasn't prepared for this kind of emergency.

Daryl handed juice boxes to some of the passengers. He saw Raymond coming and waved him over. The two stewards went to a corner of the cabin free from any passengers.

"I was thinking," said Daryl, "I think I know what that thing is."

"Yeah?"

"A werewolf."

"Come on," said Raymond.

"No, think about it. It's a full moon tonight and that thing was in a wheelchair. What kind of animal needs a wheelchair?"

Raymond didn't have an answer for that.

"And, I'm pretty sure I saw an older guy in a wheelchair get on during boarding."

"I wasn't paying attention to the back cabin."

"A werewolf," Daryl leaned in closer, "we got a fucking werewolf on the plane. You've seen the movies, right? You know what that means?"

"We need some silver bullets?"

"No . . . well, that too, but think about it. What happens when a werewolf bites someone?"

Raymond felt the blood rush out of his face. He turned and looked around a cabin full of people nursing bite wounds.

Mohammad sat in an overstuffed chair in the upper cabin. There was no enjoying the niceties of first class, not with Satan having sent a minor to thwart his mission. For what other reason could that beast be here? He saw it kill Abdul, but it would not kill him. No beast would stop him.

He stood up and walked toward the front of the cabin. The stewards had set up a service station and were offering people food, drinks, and alcohol – all free of charge. Several weak willed passengers were already passed out drunk.

He asked for an orange juice and the stewardess gave him an apologetic smile. She shook her head "no" with over-enthusiasm that made the various metal chains and rings of her uniform jingle.

"Sorry, we're all out. We do have plenty of Cucumber Pepsi and lemon vinegar Kit-Kats."

Mohammad raised an incredulous eyebrow. "No, thanks."

He turned around and headed back to his seat.

The cabin the monster had attacked was the most

populated of them all and, while the upper cabin was packed tight, it seemed like there should have been more people. He walked past two young women, their skin covered in tattoos and piercings. What little clothing they were wearing clung skin-tight to their bodies, soaked with blood.

They held each other, softly crying, and then one gently kissed the other. The kiss deepened and they began groping each other, blood soaked breasts sticking together, lip piercings tangling in their passionate embrace.

Mohammad scoffed and hurried past.

The devil really was going to great lengths to stop him but he was ordained by Allah. Nothing could get in his way.

He took his seat and leaned his head against cushioned neck rest. He closed his eyes and concentrated on the weight in his chest. Not only would he be striking a blow against a symbolic Satan, he would even be taking out one of his personal servants.

Mohammad closed his eyes and imagined the rewards awaiting him in heaven. There was no way he was letting the plane land in Portland.

"This is Fetish Flights number thirty-three we have an extreme emergency, repeat we have an extreme emergency."

The only response over the radio was static.

"Fucking nothing," said Dax.

"That's impossible," said Chavez.

As soon as the animal had started attacking, Dax and Chavez radioed a distress call to inform Portland of their situation, but they got no response. The equipment all seemed to be working fine but even when they tried radioing other planes they got only dead air. Normally, even out in the middle of the ocean, they should be able to pick up both Tokyo and Portland and at least a dozen other flights.

They both sat silent for a moment. They couldn't even count the number of flights they'd piloted together but there had never been any problems. Now that they had one, they were all alone.

"You've got to be kidding me," said Chavez.

27

"What?"

Chavez pointed at the instrument panel and Dax saw the problem immediately. The compass was spinning around wildly. Its needle pitched back and forth rapidly. The LCD readout with their speed suddenly dropped to zero and then changed to 999 and back to zero. The altitude indicator jumped up and down widely. The GPS just turned off.

The plane, however, stayed steady and gave no sign of a problem.

"We've got a real problem here," said Chavez.

Dax nodded and did the only sensible thing he could think of—he snorted another line.

"Alright," he said, "there's a monster on our plane, we lost contact with everyone, all the instruments are malfunctioning, and we still have four hours until Portland." He lit another joint, hit it, and passed it to Chavez.

He grabbed the throttle and pushed it forward. The plane picked up speed and the speakers started blaring Slayer's "Angel of Death."

"Fifty dollars says I can get us there in three and a half."

Sister Mishka Holloway realized that the infant was no longer moving. She held it out in front of her, its swathing bathed crimson. She slowly unwrapped the child and was stunned when she saw, instead of having died, the baby was completely healed. Where, just an hour before, there was a large gash, now was completely smooth pink skin.

The child's chest slowly rose up and down.

Sister began to cry. Finally after everything that had happened, God gave them a miracle.

The baby opened its eyes and looked right at her. It cooed and smiled, opening its mouth wide. That's when Sister saw its gums were bleeding. Small pointed teeth burst through the tender flesh and the child suddenly had a mouthful of needles. Its tiny body began to thrash and it sprouted a thick coat of brown fur.

She cried harder as the child transformed into something closer to an animal than human.

It leapt out of her hands and dug its tiny claws and teeth into her neck. The claws pierced her throat, grasped her windpipe and with a quick pull, wrenched it out of Sister's neck. She gurgled and fell limp. The baby werewolf giggled.

"Allah, protect me . . ." Mohammad whispered as the cabin erupted.

The low drone of people crying and talking was suddenly replaced with screams of panic and people frantically scattered in all directions. Mohammad stood up and saw fur covered monsters attacking people everywhere. It looked like anyone bitten by the beast had been similarly transformed at the exact same moment.

A very pregnant woman staggered by, her jaw missing and tongue flapping about at an odd angle. Her stomach was slashed open and the head of her unborn fetus dangled out of the wound. A werewolf pounced onto her back knocking her straight to the floor and sunk its hungry teeth into her swollen belly.

The two pierced lesbians were still making out despite the slaughter surrounding them. A monster towered over them and grabbed each one by the back of her head. It pulled them apart and then slammed them together. Their heads smashed in a soupy mixture of blood and brains.

Mohammad reached into his pockets and took out his knife and taser. He climbed over the seat in front of him while the beast gorged on the woman's corpse. A monster rushed him from his side and he shot the taser. The creature thrashed and crumpled to the floor. Another came at him from the front, climbing over a row of seats. Mohammad slashed with the knife cutting through both of its eyes.

He scanned the cabin for an escape. Everywhere, people were fighting and dying, overwhelmed by the beasts. Right next to him was the staircase leading to the lower cabins. He didn't see much of a choice, so he ran down the stairs.

Daryl was attending to an elderly woman with blue hair, two broken legs, and half her face missing from a bite when she transformed. It happened quickly and Daryl was taken off guard and didn't react. The bitch slashed forward and ripped into his pants, tearing his testicles completely off. She swung her other paw and scooped out his face as if it were nothing more than silly putty.

Raymond was across the cabin watching as, in the exact same moment, every injured person changed into a beast and assaulted their caregivers. A few tried fighting back but immediately fell to the inhuman strength of their attackers.

Above him, he heard screams and the sound of struggle from the upper cabin.

He ran to the intercom and was about to call the cockpit when he saw a passenger run to the metal door between the cabins. The man was obviously panicked and just looking for a way out when he hit the door open button. Raymond spun to stop him but he was too late.

The door slid open and the wheelchair bound werewolf burst through and ran right over the man who opened the door.

Kiichi, Kana, and Yousei were huddled by the steel door, trying to formulate a plan, when the man started screaming. They all turned to see the baby werewolf gnawing at the dead woman's neck and the injured boyfriend, now werewolf, disembowel his former love.

The body builder was just standing still, staring, and screaming like a little girl.

Both creatures immediately leapt at him and he went silent as they took him down.

"Speed Racer time," Yousei yelled as he hit the door open button.

All three punks spilled out into the back cabin. They took a quick look around but the original monster was not to be seen and the other steel door had been opened.

The boyfriend-wolf dropped the corpse and charged them. It sprung at Kana knocking her down. Kiichi immediately delivered a steel toe to the thing's temple. Yousei grabbed a suitcase from the overhead compartment and used it as a battering ram to knock the monster off Kana.

Yousei pulled her up when Kiichi noticed the The Star Spangler on the floor. He was missing both arms and a leg but he was still alive.

"A little help?" he said.

"Come on man, pogo," Kiichi said as he lifted The Star Spangler up.

"Very funny."

The Star Spangler precariously balanced himself and hopped forward on one leg. "Oh this is gonna suck."

There was a howl and they all looked back. The wheelchair-wolf was zooming straight at them. The punks climbed over the center seats leaving The Star Spangler alone in the aisle. He hopped forward as the beast gained on him. Then the footrest of the wheelchair hit him in the ankle and The Star Spangler fell on top of the monster. The two rolled forward, the beast blinded by the superhero.

The punks watched as the tangle of man and beast wheeled down the aisle and plowed straight into the wall at the end.

Kana clapped.

The werewolf pawed at The Star Spangler and grabbed a hold of his remaining leg.

"No. No. No."

The beast tore off the last purple limb and tossed it aside. It held up the torso in front of itself. The Star Spangler could see bloodlust in the monster's eyes and drool dripped down its chin. The Star Spangler had no way to defend himself, unless you counted biting and it was doubtful that would accomplish anything, but he refused to beg or cry. If this was it, he was going out with dignity.

The werewolf cocked its head and then tossed the torso aside, having lost interest in its victim.

While the monster was toying with The Star Spangler, Yousei spied Abdul's body, the taser and switchblade lying next to it. He didn't question why that man had weapons, he just grabbed them.

"Power time."

He tossed the taser to Kana and all three punks took off through the doorway into the front cabin.

They were met with a feeding frenzy. The transformed injured passengers had slaughtered their caregivers and were feasting on the corpses. Mouthful of Ants froze in the doorway. The creatures were too consumed with the carcasses to notice them.

Kiichi saw one of the flight attendants hiding behind the back rows of seats. He crouched down on the floor and was almost completely hidden from sight. Their eyes locked and the attendant held up a finger to his pursed lips. Be quiet.

Kana pushed Kiichi forward as Yousei took the lead. The three crept down the aisle. They slow stepped, careful not to draw any attention from the dozen creatures in the cabin.

They passed a werewolf that was missing the lower half of its body and lapping blood off the floor. It saw them and hunched over the puddle, growling, protecting its treat.

They got to the stairs that lead to the upper cabin and crept up them. Yousei took point so when they reached the top he signaled with this hand for them to stop. He slowly peaked his head out. To his right was the upper cabin, where apparently most of the passengers had congregated.

The room was an even bigger bloodbath than anything on the lower levels. At least two dozen werewolves were feeding, fighting, and two were even fucking amongst the seats and corpses.

As the plane pitched ever so slightly, a thick river of blood ran running down the aisle and flowed down the stairs. Kana clapped her hands over her mouth so as not to vomit, worried that the sounds of her retching would attract the beasts.

Yousei looked to the left. There were the large metal doors that led to the cockpit. Since the plane was still in the air, the pilots must still be OK. He looked back at his friends and motioned with his head in the direction of the cockpit. They nodded.

"Stay silent hill," he whispered.

He took Kana's hand and she took Kiichi's. The three slowly moved out of the stairwell into the upper cabin. Just like below, all the beasts were engaged in their own activities and took no notice of them.

They were inching toward the cockpit door when the intercom blared to life.

"This is the cockpit, can someone please respond? Is there anyone out there?"

At once all the monsters perked up and turned in the direction of the cockpit and saw the three punks.

"Fucking Jar-Jar," grumbled Kana.

"I don't get it," said Dax, "what happened to everyone?"

To punctuate his statement there was suddenly banging and muffled cries coming from their cockpit door. Dax and Chavez both looked back.

"Well let them in," said Dax.

Chavez got up and unlocked the door. He opened it and three young people decked out in black leather, multi-colored hair, and covered in piercings and tattoos spilled in. Behind them, from floor to ceiling was a wall of brown fur, claws, and gnashing teeth.

He slammed the door shut and the monsters slammed into it. The door shook but the strong steel did not budge.

Dax turned and looked at the punks getting to their feet and saw that Chavez's face had gone white.

"Dude . . . what's up?"

Chavez sat back down at the controls and took the joint from Dax. He hit it long and hard.

"Will one of you tell me what the fuck is happening?"

"Mega mecha werewolf horde," gasped the female punk.

Chavez stared at the punk and passed her the joint.

"Rasta," she, said grinning.

Chavez turned to Dax, "I'm way too high for this shit."

3
WEREWOLVES ON A PLANE

Mohammad climbed over the bodies in the back cabin. He found it surprisingly easy to get back there. Most of the monsters were too concerned with their kills and those punks distracted the others leaving him free to move about the lower section of the plane.

He searched through the bodies and found Abdul. His friend was mangled with most of his insides now outside. The upper part of his chest was untouched. Mohammad found the hidden button and Abdul's chest flipped open. Inside were the explosives, still armed and operational.

Mohammad was relieved. Allah was still watching over him.

He removed the bomb as he heard howls from the upper deck and the sound of heavy creatures moving about. The punks must have gotten the monsters excited and they were searching for more prey they may have overlooked.

He pulled out the bomb and looked around. He headed to the bathrooms and service station at the back of the cabin. The area was empty, with the exception of two mutilated corpses.

He pushed the button shutting the emergency doors and slumped to the ground. His body was sore and tired but he was still alive.

On the floor next to him was a small one-foot-wide hole that had been torn into the aircraft's floor. He paid no mind.

Raymond was still hiding in the seats when he heard the horde moving down the stairs. The werewolves were on the move. Those damn punks must have gotten them excited.

The beasts began to flow down the stairs into the cabin, sniffing the air and growling.

Raymond knew he had to get out of there.

He crawled beneath the seat in front of him. He didn't know where he was going. The cockpit crossed his mind but all the monsters were blocking the stairwells. Then his back bumped into a seat and the fetish wear on his uniform rattled. A growl sounded next to his ear. He turned, and there, still sitting in the wheelchair, was the damn beast that started this all.

Raymond got to his feet and backed away from the snarling creature. His back hit the wall and he found himself next to the emergency exit.

Then a crazy idea crossed his mind.

He looked around the cabin and there looked to be fifty werewolves staring back at him. Each one drooling and eyeing him with desire.

He reached his hands back and found the emergency lock. He clicked it off.

His movements were slow and calm, he didn't want to excite them just yet. The pack crept forward. The wheelchair wolf held its position in front of him and continued to growl.

Raymond paused for a moment and tried to think of something positive, some good last note to go out on. But he had nothing. He had no family. No love in his life. His career and constant travel had made keeping even basic friendships impossible. Hell, his cat died last year.

He looked around the cabin as the monsters bore down on him.

"Fuck ya'll," he whispered and opened the door.

"Mother-cunt-fucker. What now?" Dax yelled as alarms went off all over the cockpit. The punks were sitting on the floor and the five had been passing joints around constantly. The punks were kind of weird, especially how they talked, but he and Chavez did manage to find out from them that the plane was filled with werewolves and, most likely, they were the only five people left alive.

But there was a bigger problem. He knew Chavez noticed it as well but hadn't said anything. One of the few instruments that will still working was their odometer. According to it, they should be over the west coast of the United States right now with Portland just a scant half an hour away. Instead, open ocean and black skies stretched out for forever in front of them. Even if the odometer was malfunctioning and even if they weren't going as fast as they thought, land should be in sight.

Dawn was also due forty minutes ago.

"We got decompression in the front cabin," responded Chavez

"What's our altitude?"

"You know damn well the altimeter is not working."

"Shit, OK let's hope we can do this." Dax snorted another line. "Hold on," he directed as he began to take the plane down.

If they didn't get the plane below 20,000 feet in a matter of minutes the entire plane would depressurize, exposing them all to extreme cold and a dangerous lack of oxygen. They would be knocked unconscious.

When Raymond opened the door, it flipped outward with such force that it surprised him. He suddenly found himself outside the plane hanging onto the door handle. His body pressed flat against the plane.

Monsters, corpses, and luggage flew out from the doorway in a constant stream. Raymond screamed, not in terror but primal rage at the beasts. Now they were the ones dying.

He saw the monster in the wheelchair come flying out with the other debris.

Got you, you bastard.

He pulled with all his strength toward the doorway. He had resigned himself to dying when he opened the door but now he was willing to fight for survival again.

He felt the plane pitch down and the pull became less strong. Dax and Chavez must still be alive and they were trying to pressurize the plane. There was still a chance of making it out of this.

Through the grace of God he managed to pull himself into the doorway. He held onto the doorframe tight and the plane kept going lower. He looked into the cabin and it seemed to be empty of almost everything. The oxygen masks had lowered and were whipping about from the overhead compartment.

There was something bouncing around in the cabin. Raymond struggled to make out the shiny purple blur. It suddenly was headed straight at him and then he heard the blur screaming.

It shot straight at him and Raymond was able to register the blur as a torso with a screaming head right before it hit him square in the chest. The force sent him and what was left of The Star Spangler out into open air.

Dax leveled the plane when he reached what he thought was a low enough altitude. There was no real way to be sure. But they were not knocked out, so he must have been successful.

"I think we're OK," said Dax.

One of the punks shushed him.

The cockpit got quiet and they all listened. Beneath the floor came a strange scratching sound.

"What the hell is that?" asked Chavez.

Suddenly, all the instruments in the cockpit began sounding alarms or just shutting off.

"We've got massive failure across the board. We're losing control of all vital systems," Dax informed.

A hole burst open in the floor and a small furry blur burst out. The baby werewolf began bouncing around the cockpit like a basketball slashing and biting. All five started screaming and blindly striking at the creature.

Kana took out the taser and struck forward. The beast squealed and hopped on top of the instrument panel. It giggled and its claws dug into the controls, damaging them even more. Chavez smacked it with the back of his hand and the little monster grabbed their bag of coke and dove back into the hole it emerged from.

"What the fuck just happened?"

"I think a baby werewolf just stole our coke."

"This is getting stupid!"

Kana grabbed Dax and started shaking his shoulder to get his attention. She was pointing frantically out the window toward the left wing of the plane.

Dax squinted, trying to see what was going on. "There's . . . something . . . on the wing of the plane."

He could see a large blob on the wing of the plane but he couldn't make sense of what he was looking at. The lights on the wing blinked on an off briefly illuminating it. He saw what it was but it took his brain a moment to make sense of it.

The werewolf in the wheelchair was on the wing, somehow staying in place. The wind whipped the thing's fur against its body. The beast howled at the moon and Dax swore he heard it above the noise of the plane.

The beast began to tear into the wing, prying back paneling and attacking wires.

"Oh . . . oh, this is so bad," said Chavez right before the plane started violently rocking side to side.

"OK," said Dax. He took his hands off the steering joystick and sat back examining his ruined instrument panel. He pushed a button and the speakers blasted, "Ziggy Stardust" by David Bowie.

He felt surprisingly calm as he lit up what he knew was his last joint. "Try to hold onto something. We're going down."

"Let's rock and roll," Yousei nervously said.

Mohammad woke up in the hallway. He must have passed out from exhaustion. He could feel the plane going down.

He assumed that he had slept through the rest of the trip and that they were landing in Portland. This was what he was waiting for. He pulled up his shirt and opened the hidden compartment in his chest. He armed the bomb and closed his eyes, saying a silent prayer.

There was a screeching sound and he opened his eyes to see a miniature werewolf coming out of the hole in the floor. Some kind of white powered was covering its snout.

"Praise be to Allah," he said and the bomb went off.

***

In the cockpit they heard and felt the explosion. The plane was only a few yards above the water when the bomb blew. The cabin split open and the cockpit was sent rocketing forward, flipping over.

Kiichi saw Chavez's chest cave-in as he was thrown into the steering joystick.

The punks went bouncing around the cockpit and Kiichi tried to reach out to one of his friends but his head hit the ceiling and the world went black.

Kiichi was aware of the wet and the cold but nothing else. Then he felt open air and his lungs gasped for oxygen.

He opened his eyes to see Kana and Yousei leaning down over him, grinning.

"Nine lives," said Kana.

"Like a mongoose," said Yousei laughing.

Kiichi shook his head and regained his senses. He sat up and looked around. The three punks floated atop an inflatable emergency raft. About a hundred yards away, the burning wreckage of the plane was slowly sinking below the waves.

"Flyboys?" he asked.

Kana shook her head. "No."

He grimly nodded. At least the three of them had made it.

High above them, the full moon illuminated the open ocean and the last bit of wreckage sunk beneath the water.

Yousei started shouting and pointing. Kana and Kiichi turned and looked in the direction of his finger. Through the darkness they saw another raft drifting in their direction and there appeared to be someone on it.

All three began yelling and waving, they were so happy they weren't the only survivors.

The other raft drifted closer and all three punks fell silent when they got a good look at it. In the center of the raft, still sitting in the wheelchair, was the cripple wolf. It howled at the moon and waved its paws eagerly in their direction, like it was trying to will them closer – and it was working.

The two rafts were approaching each other at a quicker speed. The punks dropped to their knees and tried in vain to paddle with their hands in the opposite direction but the cruel ocean currents were too strong.

In moments the two rafts were touching and the werewolf lunged forward, falling off its wheelchair but directly on top of Yousei. He screamed as the werewolf tore into his stomach. Kana jumped on the beast and pulled out the taser. She tried to shock it but weapon was soaked with salt water and rendered useless.

The wolf reached back and grabbed the top of her head with its powerful paw.

Kiichi rushed the creature and it lazily backhanded him, sending him flying through the air right onto the other raft. He sat up and Kana's shrieks reached an unnatural pitch. He managed to get to his feet just in time to see the beast pop Kana's head from her body.

He froze in shock and the beast tossed her corpse overboard. He noticed that Yousei was still alive and moving but for some reason he was smiling. Yousei's hand made a quick motion and something metal flew through the air toward Kiichi. He caught the object and looked down to see he was holding the switchblade they found onboard the plane.

The sudden movement attracted the werewolf's attention and it turned to face Kiichi. The punk flicked the blade open and moonlight glimmered off the weapon.

Yousei flashed him devil horns, "Rock and roll forever."

Kiichi returned the sign, "Party every night."

The werewolf howled and slashed Yousei's neck, finishing the kill.

Kiichi flipped the weapon in the air, caught it by the blade, and whipped the knife straight at the center of the raft. There was a loud *Pop* and the raft quickly began to deflate. The beast saw what was happening and frantically began to try and crawl back to the other raft where its chair was. Its movements only pushed the air out faster.

Yousei's corpse went beneath the water and the monster

thrashed about with its arms. Its legs hung useless and the beast slipped beneath the waves.

Kiichi looked over the side of the raft and watched the monster desperately try to doggie paddle, its muscular arms and wet fur slapping against the water. Bubbles erupted to the surface as it lost its struggle and sunk below the waves. Then the ocean was quiet and Kiichi was alone.

He collapsed. His body was weak and soaked to the bone. He rolled over and threw up, his nerves beyond shot. With great effort, he managed to sit up. The monster's wheelchair still sat on the raft. He snorted in disgust at it and pushed the contraption over the side into the water.

Far off in the horizon, the first rays of the long-delayed dawn finally broke, the sky just beginning to turn the deepest shade of purple. When the first stabs of yellow pierced the sky, Kiichi began to laugh and cry.

HHHHHOOOOONNNNNKKKKK

Kiichi turned around. Not more than a few hundred meters away was a small fishing ship. He waved at the vessel and lay back down in the raft.

Now he was just laughing. He survived. He would live to see another day.

He felt so good that he didn't even notice the bite wound on his ankle.

41

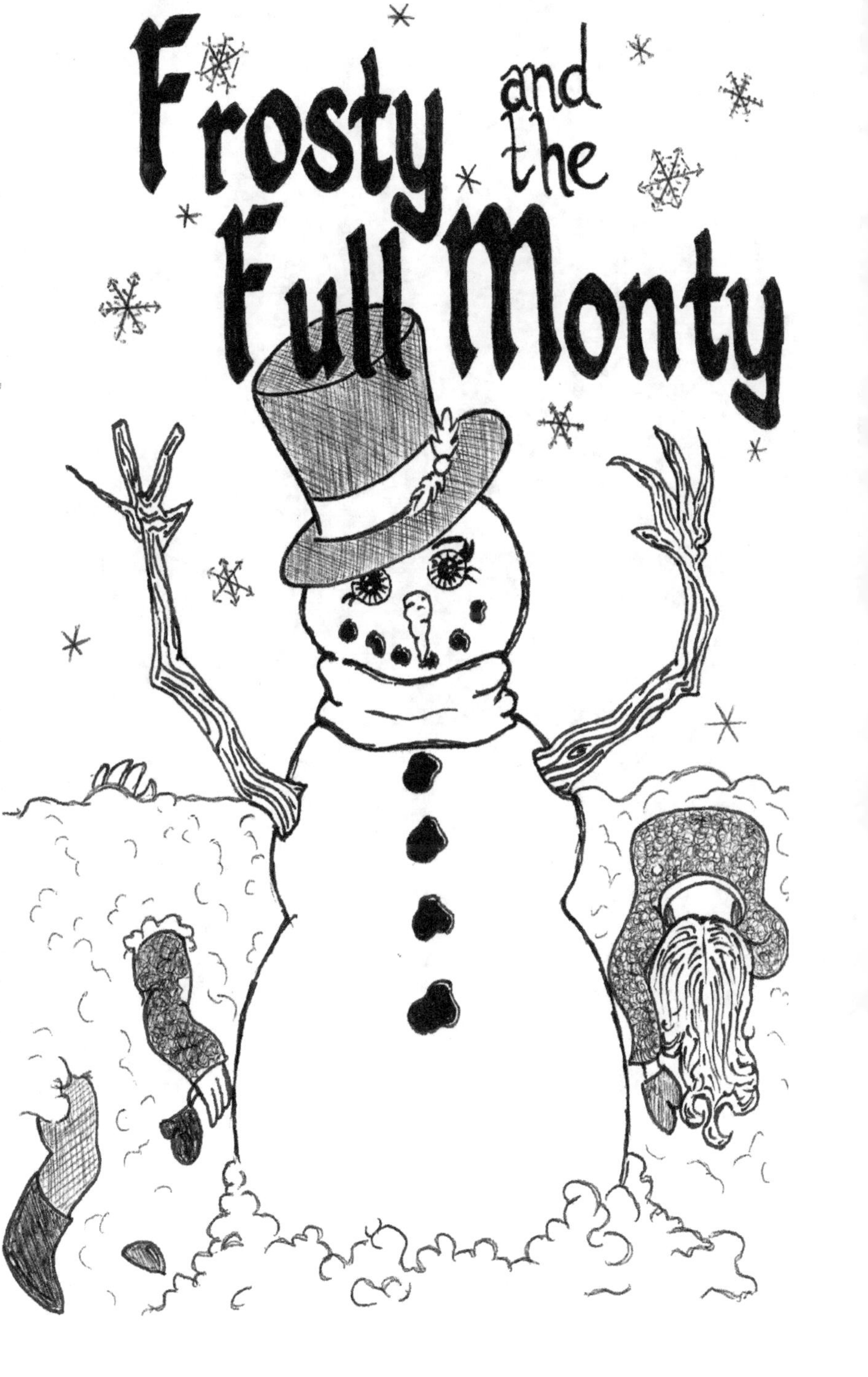
Frosty and the Full Monty

Frosty the Snowman stepped onto the stage for the third time that night. With one icy hand he grabbed the stripper pole and swung his hips to Bing Crosby's voice crooning over the club's PA system.

A gang of bikers crowded the club. Every seat was filled with tattooed, leather jacketed, pierced members of The Crack Pipe Kings Motorcycle Club. They had been here all night, just like last night and the night before.

Frosty didn't know why they were always there. He figured they liked the girls of the club and he was a *snowman.* But he seemed to be their favorite and they did tip very well.

The stage lights illuminated his snow body and the crowd went wild. They cheered, clanked beers, and head butted each other in excitement.

Frosty the snowman was a jolly happy soul.

Blue sequin bikini briefs glittered in the spotlight on his pelvis. The light was hot and Frosty could feel his snow beginning to melt. Fortunately, his dances were only four minutes long.

He began to dance around.

That was his cue. He turned slowly, facing the audience, reached down sliding his finger under the special Velcro strap and quickly tore off the briefs revealing his smooth snowman physique. Frosty ground his hips against the pole and the audience roared.

Karen, Jackie, Billy and June were building a magnificent snowman. He was almost as tall as the stop sign he was next to. They had given him two pieces of coal for eyes, a red button for a nose, and even a corncob pipe.

The last touch was the black silk hat that Karen had found. It was hard to reach, but with help from Jackie and Billy, Karen got the hat on top of the snowman's head.

All four children stepped back to admire their creation— straight into the path of an oncoming snowplow. The driver wasn't paying that close of attention, he was shitfaced. All four bodies were very small so there wasn't even a thump as they got overtaken by snow and pushed by the plow. They

45

were crushed into a large mound of ice and their bodies weren't discovered for two weeks.

It turns out there was a little magic in that old silk hat they found. The snowman they had built leapt to life and began to dance around.

A bum walking by yelled "Yay! It's Frosty!"

Frosty waved back. "Good day, Sir."

He went walking down the street, as happy as could be. Everyone waved at him and shouted greetings as he strolled by.

He came to an alleyway and there was a very skinny man wearing a very dirty trench coat leaning against the wall.

"Good day, Sir," said Frosty.

The man, whose name was Alan, beamed the biggest smile he had in years. Instantly, he was transported back to those childhood Christmases and remembered how in-between his dad beating him and putting out cigarettes on his arms, he would escape into the magic of those television specials: *Rudolph the Red Nosed Reindeer*, *A Garfield Christmas* and his favorite, *Frosty the Snowman*.

So Alan offered Frosty the one thing he had.

"Hey Frosty, wanna do some ice?"

Frosty assumed, since he was a snowman, that "ice" must be something good for him. He did not know what was being offered was methamphetamine.

Frosty hit the pipe and the drug went straight to his head and heart. Euphoria overtook him, he loved it! As it turns out, snowmen are quite addition prone. Frosty was instantly addicted.

Bing Crosby stopped singing and the PA began to blast The Beach Boys rendition of "Frosty the Snowman." The sweet sixties pop had been specially remixed by the Club's DJ to include a booty-shaking, boot-stomping bass line.

The bikers cheered louder, this was their favorite song for Frosty to dance to and every set he did ended this way.

A skinny and sickly looking biker climbed onto the stage and rushed at Frosty. His lust making him forget proper club decorum.

From the shadows, two obese bouncers moved with surprising agility grabbing the biker. They lifted him up, one putting him in a headlock and the other grabbing his legs. They carried him off the stage and through a door. The stage invader would be found in the hospital the next morning. This was not the first time the club had aggressively enforced the no-touching rule. It was that kind of club.

The rest of the gang paid him no mind, their beer-and-boner-goggles keeping them enraptured with Frosty and his stage show.

So Frosty spent his days smoking and hanging in alleys with other bums and wastes of life, and it was a happy time. Each day blended into the next in his drug haze and Alan and Frosty became the best of friends.

But one day the money ran out and Frosty and Alan found themselves with handguns holding up a liquor store. The store clerk had a shotgun. The first shot took Alan's head clean off, splattering the snowman with blood and brains. But when the clerk turned the gun on Frosty, the buckshot passed through Frosty's torso of snow with no ill effect.

Frosty fired back and ran, leaving the clerk to bleed out. In a short time he was caught. The red stained snow made it an open and shut case.

On his first day in federal prison, he was cornered by a group of Crips. They mistook the blood stains in his snow for Frosty reppin' the wrong colors. They formed a circle around him and pushed him back and forth hurling insults. In the jostle his hat got knocked off and Frosty immediately turned back into a plain old snowman.

When a guard finally put his hat back on, Frosty found himself covered in sticky, white goo. After a trip to the med ward and a few meetings with the prison counselor, Frosty understood what happened to him.

That was how he learned to perform "snowjobs."

He used this peculiar talent to get through his time in prison. He was able to trade snowjobs for protection, smokes, and when the prison served ice cream, extra dessert.

This gift to leave his body proved vital for the survival of a snowman who, for some unknown reason, aroused the lust of the biggest and meanest inmates.

Frosty sat in his private freezer/dressing room. The club owner had been nice enough to build a special room for Frosty to refreeze his snow after every dance.

Frosty took a drag from a cigarette and placed it into the ashtray on his dresser. He looked at his reflection in the mirror. The years had been hard on him; his once pure white snow was now an ugly grey.

In front of the mirror was his only personal possession, the corncob pipe he came to life with. He thought of all he had been through and all he had smoked with that pipe; meth, crack, marijuana, and on the rare occasion, tobacco.

There was a knock at the door and Cinnamon poked her head in.

"You got a private customer in booth three," she said and shut the door.

Frosty sighed and took a hit of ice from his corncob pipe.

He stood up and left the room. The private booths were just down the hall, each one labeled one through six. Frosty walked into number three.

Eventually his sentence was up and Frosty's debt to society was paid. But what was a living snowman with no job skills and a criminal record to do?

He found that his snowjob skill from prison had use on the outside as well. In no time at all, Frosty was trading snowjobs for his precious ice.

One day he was lying in an alley, the same alley where so many years ago he met Alan, stoned out of his head, when a fat greasy man walked by. The man stopped when he saw the snowman. This man owned *Jezebel's* the city's most notorious strip club.

He had been looking for something new for the club, something to revive customer interest and looking at the down-on-his-luck snowman, he had an idea.

The man helped Frosty to his feet.

"Hey kid, I gotta business proposition for you."

The booth was small, barely enough room for the burly biker and the portly snowman. The walls were lined with mirrors and a single bare light bulb hung from the ceiling.

Over the room's private speakers, Alvin and the Chipmunks were singing.

And the children say he could laugh and play just the same as you and me.

That damn song. It didn't matter what time of year or what month it was. His customers always requested the same song. Sometimes different artists—The Jackson 5, The Ronettes, Ella Fitzgerald, Cocteau Twins, Fiona Apple—but always the same damn song.

Frosty wondered all the time about the song. Was there another snowman that came to life before him? Was that one lucky to lead a happy life? Or was it really about him? Everyone did call him "Frosty."

The biker stood up and approached Frosty. No matter how hard he tried, Frosty never got used to this. He felt the heat of the lightbulb above his head. A tear ran from his button eye but was indistinguishable from the just-beginning-to-form slush.

The biker kissed Frosty softly on his lips of coal. Flecks of snow dotted his bushy beard. He gently removed Frosty's hat and unbuckled his pants, preparing for his snowjob.

BLACK SCREEN

Male narrator with a deep voice: In the year 3012 mankind faced its most dire crisis. As the world's population approached eighteen billion, the legalization and encouragement of cannibalism solved many concerns of food shortages and overpopulation. This created a booming demand for chefs of all kinds. There were so many people in the world and so much food that needed cooking.

But then came the crash—there ended up being just too many chefs.

Screen flashes images of bustling, packed cities from all over the world. The streets are filled with dirty and broken people wearing chef hats and aprons. The camera lingers on a man holding a cardboard sign that reads, "Will Sauté for Food."

Narrator: With so many people vying to cook, some method of selection had to be implemented. An arena was created for contestants to prove themselves worthy of serving the world. That battlefield is called . . .

Off screen an audience yells in unison: "*Cook . . . For . . . Your . . . Life!*"

Loud applause and cheering. Screen displays the show's logo—a red background with the silhouettes of two crossed butcher knives. COOK FOR is above the blades, with YOUR LIFE below.

The studio lights kicked on and Amy thought she'd died and gone to the great bistro in the sky—the brightness momentarily blinding, before her eyes adjusted. She'd waited and wished for so long to be standing there that she had started to doubt the moment would ever come—but there she was. On *Cook for Your Life!*

She stood in a kitchenette with a sink, stove top, blender, plenty of counter space, and a menagerie of pots, pans and cooking utensils. A black board that read "Amy" in red LCD floated ten feet above the cooking space. Off to the side, almost completely hidden in the shadows, a guard gripped a machine gun.

Just like on TV. The viewers are probably seeing our intro videos right now!

She spun around to take in the room and examine the four other kitchenettes. Above each, a giant spotlight brightly illuminated the space. The five kitchenettes were spread apart like the points of a star. In the center stood a huge empty table. Somewhere in the darkness of the cavernous room hummed the television cameras, broadcasting this contest to billions around the world.

The other four contestants were taking in the situation as well. Directly across from Amy was a man that could pass for a professional body-builder. Dressed in a shining silver suit that covered his entire body, hands and feet included, only leaving his neck and head exposed. His head spins, not turns but spins like Regan in the Exorcist, and Amy realized that he's not wearing a suit—his body was metal. A cyborg. She had heard of people that underwent the procedure but she had never seen one in person—just on screen. His display read "Sliceatron."

Damn—he's even a cooking model.

In the space to her right was a man in black dress pants, a white button-up shirt, and a black tie to match. He looked scared shitless. Amy knew his story right away—it happens. The selecting machines aren't too picky, the basic assumption is *everybody* wants to be a chef and sometimes the machine zaps some poor sap who is one of the few that doesn't want to cook for a living. His display said "Josh."

He'll be out first round.

The next chef was a monkey—or a gorilla to be correct. The ape stood calmly, looking around taking in the situation. On its head was a helmet with a mess of blinking lights and wires. The beast saw Amy looking and waved. Amy waved back.

I hate the monkey-people.

Above the gorilla's kitchenette, the screen said "Mindy."

Amy looked to the last kitchenette and didn't see anyone there. The name screen read "Buffo," but the space appeared empty.

Odd name.

She moved a few steps to the left and craned her head. A knee poked out from behind the table. The contestant was sitting on the ground and the big table was blocking her view. She moved over more to get a good look and her heart skipped a beat.

—oh shit.

A clown sat cross-legged on the ground. His eyes were closed in deep mediation with his white gloved hands held in front, palm up. In one hand sat a seltzer bottle, in the other a hand-buzzer. The red and yellow polka-dotted pants, Hawaiian shirt, sky-blue jacket, white face-paint, and red foam nose clashed with the serene state he projected.

Amy recognized his clothing right away—he was a follower of the Clown School of Cooking. The most feared of all the secret cooking sects, no follower had ever lost an episode of "Cook for Your Life."

A massive television screen flashed on in the darkness high above the cooking area. A small Japanese woman wearing a gaudy blue plastic suit and plastic police cap waved and stared straight at the camera.

"Konichiwa chefs! Please assume your positions, the show is about to begin. *Tee-hee*." She curtsied and the screen turned off.

Amy rushed over to her cooking space, leaned back against the counter, and looked up. Lowering down from the darkness was the Supreme Chef.

Like a God or Q on *Star Trek: The Next Generation*, the Supreme Chef floated down from the rafters riding a great levitating throne of black steel. He wore a red cloak of the finest cheese-cloth, intricately detailed with pin-point stitching of great cooking battles throughout history—the Acacius/Bion wine grape stomp-out, the Tyson/Simpson grilled cheese cook-off, and more.

At his side was a sheathed sword—the legendary Blade-O-Matic 5600. The sword was the greatest cutlery known to man and only the most worthy could wield it. Whoever controlled the sword was the greatest chef in the world, the master of flavor itself.

The Supreme Chef spoke and his voice boomed over speakers hidden somewhere in the shadows, "Chefs, you have been selected today to have your chance at what you've always dreamed of—your own restaurant! The winner of today's contest will have the opportunity to select any kitchen, anywhere in the world, as their prize. It will be theirs until the end of their days—or until somebody else selects that prize."

He floated around the room inspecting each of the contestants. As he approached Amy, she met his eyes and smirked. He grinned back.

"You will compete today in a series of trials," he continued, "designed to prove which of you is worthiest of serving the world. There will be four rounds. At the end of each round, one chef will be eliminated. The last cook left standing will be the winner.'

ROUND 1

The screen flashed on and the girl was back, "alright, let's get this show started! For round one you will each prove your basic knowledge of food and—as we all know—the basic building block of any person's diet is . . . people!"

Above each of the kitchenettes, a slab lowered down from the ceiling. On each slab was a full-grown, recently dead human corpse.

A body came to a stop next to Amy's counters. There was no obvious cause of death and it did not look like any decay had set in—a beautiful hunk of meat that would run Amy at least one year's wage if she were to buy it on the open market.

The video girl continued, "any decent chef should know basic butchery and that's what your first challenge will be testing.

"The liver is a relatively easy to identify and access organ of the human body. It is also a favorite of many upscale restaurants in the finer parts of the City. If you win today's competition, you will surely be asked to remove a liver at some point.

"When the Supreme Chef gives the signal, cut into your body and remove the liver. The first four contestants that complete the challenge will advance to the next round. The fifth will be eliminated.

"Good luck!"

The screen went black.

The Supreme Chef floated to the center of the room and hovered there for a moment. He surveyed all of the contenders and then yelled, "*Allez cuisine!*"

A loud mechanical whirling and buzzing issued from the Sliceatron kitchenette. Sliceatron was already holding up a liver and his body was nothing more than a pile of red slush. Amy hadn't even made the first cut yet.

Of course a cyborg named "Sliceatron" does well in the butchery round.

She turned her attention to the task at hand. On the slab next to the corpse, she neatly laid out a selection of utensils: a cleaver, scalpel, boning knife, filet knife, and a rib spreader.

Time was of the essence, so she grabbed the cleaver, raised it above her head, and sunk the blade into the breast between the pectorals. With some effort she pulled the blade out and hacked down again and again. Soon there was a wide gash in the body from the upper chest down to the belly button. Fortunately the body wasn't too fresh and the blood had congealed. Nothing is messier that working on a fresh kill.

She grabbed the rib spreader, insert its prongs into the gash, grabbed hold of the crank, and—

CRACK!

The chest bloomed open. It was just a matter of finding the liver and cutting it out.

Piece of cake.

Amy knew she needed to focus but she couldn't help checking out the competition. She looked over at Buffo— she had always wanted to see a clown in action. Surprisingly, he was not holding any kind of cutting implement. Instead, he placed his hands on the center of his corpse's abdomen. His head upturned and his eyes tightly shut.

Suddenly, his arms disappeared up to his elbows into the body. Amy froze in her work, fascinated by what she was seeing. Buffo moved about as he dug deeper into the body. Then he smoothly removed both arms. With one hand he hit his button, with the other he held up a perfectly removed liver. Most interesting, the body showed no sign of damage—no cuts, gashes, or tears, despite the fact that Buffo had its liver.

The clowns live up to their hype thought Amy. *That just leaves me, the monkey, and Josh.*

She snuck a look at Josh who just stood and stared at the corpse in front of him.

Gotta concentrate.

Amy went back to work. She already had the chest cavity spread wide and had easy access to the main internal organ structure. It was just a matter of sifting around and—

—there you are.

She found the liver. She reached over and grabbed a scalpel from the knife spread. With a few quick cuts, the meat was free. She hit the button and held the organ over her head.

"Wooooo!" she yelled and jumped up and down.

Now that she was finished, Amy could watch the others. The gorilla had a cleaver in each hand and indiscriminately hacked away at the torso in front of it (for some reason the beast already cut off and discarded the body's arms, legs, and head).

Then Mindy tossed both blades aside and dug into the chest cavity with her bare paws. Her arm jerked as she pulled and twisted to loosen the organ. When she got it free, Mindy held the liver over her head and hit the button. She jumped up and down and hooted in gorilla joy.

That only left—

The Supreme Chef hovered over to Josh. He sat on the floor of his kitchenette with tears streaming down his face. He held one of the knives the show had supplied— incidentally, one way too small for the task he was given. His meat was unharmed except for one small three-inch cut across the lower abdomen; he wasn't even going to cut into the right part of the body.

"I . . . can't. I don't even want to be a chef," pleaded Josh.

The Supreme Chef looked down at him but gave no hint of emotion.

"Please . . . I just want to go home."

The Supreme Chef spoke, "Josh you are the one white bean in a can of baked beans—disappointing and meant to be discarded. You didn't entertain our audience but you'll still get your chance to be a star. *Torisaru!*"

At once, all the spotlights in the room turned dark except for the light above Josh—his turned deep red. A loud buzzer pierced their ears and a blinding flash of white light washed over them.

Amy shielded her eyes with her hands and, when she lowered them, Josh was gone.

The video screen flickered on.

"Oh, poor Josh," said the Japanese girl with mock sympathy, "he blew his chance here but he'll still be super *tasty!* He's going to be the special guest on another wonderful show on this network—Sweet Sixteen BBQ!"

The image on the screen changed to a human corpse slow roasting over a pit of fire. The flesh so well cooked that it was impossible to tell what the person originally looked like or even if they were a man or woman. A pole skewers it from asshole to mouth holding the body in place as it slowly rotated over the open flames. Around the cooking pit a bunch of teenage girls wore party hats and held plates of birthday cake. They couldn't seem to care less about the still-cooking meal.

The image cuts back to the video girl, "Let's hope he's more *satisfying* on that show than he was here."

COMMERCIAL BREAK

(*Interior: inside of tree house with three boys sitting around reading comic books. A forth boy climbs in waving a book. He starts speaking excitedly*)

Boy 1: Hey guys, have you read *Shatnerquake* by Jeff Burk yet?

Boy 2: I have! It's super!

Boy 3: It's Shatnertastic!

Boy 4: I never knew William Shatner was so tough.

Boy 1, now fully inside the tree house and sitting in the circle with the other boys: I know, I don't think anyone could beat him up.

Voice off screen: Now boys, don't believe everything you read.

(*The boys spin around and the camera shows William Shatner climbing into the tree house.*)

All four boys in unison: William Shatner!

William Shatner: I know *Shatnerquake* is amazing but it's just a story. I am not a

master of Shaolin-Style Street Fighting,
I don't speak like a stroke victim, and
I've never fought a light-saber wielding
Captain Kirk with a Bat'leth.

All four boys hang their heads in union:
Ooohhhhh . . .

William Shatner: But the book did get one
thing right.

All four boys look up excited and say in
unison: What?

William Shatner: I drink the blood of
young runaways.

(*William Shatner hisses and opens his mouth
wider than humanly possible revealing
long dagger-like teeth. The camera zooms
in on the gaping maw as the boys scream.*)

ROUND 2

The video girl blinked on. "For your second challenge, you
will be working with one of the all time classic deserts—ice
cream!"

A large tray lowered down from the darkness of the
ceiling onto the center table. In the center of the tray mounds
of chocolate ice cream filled a huge bowl. Around the edges
of the tray were smaller bowls over-flowing with every ice
cream topping imaginable.

"You will have two minutes," continued the girl, "using
only the items on the table, to make the best sundae possible.
Whoever does not measure up will be eliminated!"

The Supreme Chef floated into the middle of the room,
hovering above the table, and his voice boomed, "Round
two, *Allez cuisine!*"

The contestants raced to the center of the room to start the challenge. Amy grabbed a scoop and an empty bowl and served two generous dollops. She surveyed the toppings—whipped cream, bananas, sprinkles (chocolate and rainbow), gummy bears, mini M&M's, salted peanuts, and chocolate drops. Amy had only a moment to consider and decided on all of them.

Judging from how the others were grabbing—they all had the same plan.

In no time, the buzzers went off, signifying that their time was up. Amy had a mess in the bowl but it looked like a pretty tasty mess.

The video said, "alight contestants, ready? We have a very special guest for this round—the ten year old child-star sensation, Shirley Sunshine! Star of such blockbusters as "Honey I Blew the Kids," "Big Trouble in Little Vagina," and many others."

On the far side of the room, a giant door opened in the shadows letting in blinding amounts of white light and a healthly dose of dry ice fog. A silhouette of a small girl skipped into the arena and the door closed behind her.

The girl bobbed her way into the main light. Her curly red hair bouncing as she walked. Dressed in a poufy and frilly dress, she looked like any other little girl, but for the heavy and dark bags under her eyes and the track marks on her arms. She arrived at the center display of ice cream and the dull, glazed look in her eyes lifted.

"Good evening Shirley, are you ready for some ice cream?"

The girl nodded and visually salivated.

"Sliceatron, present your creation."

The Cyborg handed his sundae over and Amy's mouth dropped open. The ice cream was smoothed out on the bottom of the dish providing a base for a diorama he'd created of two dozen gummy bears reenacting the Battle of Gettysburg.

The girl paid little attention to the elaborate display and dug in viciously, her spoon doing more damage than any gummy cannon could even hope. After a few greedy spoonfuls, she put the bowl back on the table and announced, "Next!"

"Amy, you're up," said the video girl.

Amy handed her mess of a dessert to the little girl. She took two tiny mouthfuls and her eyes wandered over to leftovers of Sliceatron's display.

"I like the sprinkles in the gun wounds," she said. *Oh, shit. This isn't going well.*

She took a few more weak bites and then put the bowl back on the table. "Next!"

"OK, Buffo, you're up," said the video girl.

The clown bounded over to the girl with an exaggerated wobble to his step and a comically huge smile on his face. He got down on one knee and presented the bowl to the girl. The sundae looked average—nothing special about it at all.

As Shirley ate, Buffo produced a handful of balloons from some hidden pocket. He stretched one out and began to blow it up. He twisted and knotted the long narrow balloon into the shape of a sword.

The girl shoveled in the ice cream while she watched mesmerized. As she took her next bite, Buffo poked her in the belly with the sword and she giggled. She put the ice cream on the table and clapped, "Next!"

This was not looking good for Amy. *I just hope that monkey fucks up.*

"OK Mindy, you're the final competitor this round," said the video girl.

Shirley walked over to the gorilla and the beast bent down over the bowl. She took it, patted Mindy on the nose, and giggled.

She took a spoonful of ice cream, stuck it in her mouth, and froze. The expression on her face went from happy, to confused, to enraged. She threw down the spoon and spit the ice cream out of her mouth.

"What the fuck is this shit?" she screamed and threw the bowl at Mindy. The gorilla flinched as the dish bounced off its shoulder.

"You tryin' to poison me?" Shirley started digging around her mouth with one hand.

"I mean, what the fuck is this shit?" With two fingers she pulled a long strand of hair from between her teeth. "Monkey hair? Monkey hair! Fuck!"

Shirley turned from Mindy and marched away from the contest. The door in the wall opened back up and she walked through it. As she did, she flipped her middle finger at the contestants and yelled, "Mindy, you lose."

The Supreme Chef flew over to the gorilla and hung in the air before her.

"Haha, silly monkey, you have technique but no skill. The other contestants are fresh slices from a New York Pizzeria—you are frozen and reheated in the oven. *Torisaru!*"

Red light poured over Mindy as the rest of the room darkened.

BBBUUUZZZZZZ!!!!

The gorilla disappeared and the screen flickered back on. The image showed the gorilla strapped onto a table with its head poking though. A team of surgeons, armed with a variety of medical instruments, sliced and diced the metal cap, and top of Mindy's skull. A few quick cuts and Mindy convulsed as the medical team scooped out the animal's brain.

"Oh Mindy," said the video girl over the footage, "you'll now have forever to get serving ice cream right."

The team cleaned out Mindy's skull and one of the surgeons produced a tub of ice cream. He took two scoops of vanilla and placed them neatly in the skull with a sprig of mint for a garnish.

The medical team quickly disappeared from view and a fat, expensively dressed woman appeared and sat down at the table. She daintily produced a spoon and began to eat the desert with great relish.

COMMERCIAL BREAK

(Interior of a dirty empty room. The walls are gray stone and the floor is concrete. A single bare bulb hangs down overhead illuminating the scene. A young blonde *woman is on her knees. Duct tape covers her mouth. The viewer cannot see, but it is obvious from her struggle her feet and hands are bound behind her. Her nose is coated with dried blood and one of her eyes is swollen and black. Her clothes are torn and dirtied; she's been through a lot.*

Next to her is a skinny man with long hair. He is wearing faded blue jeans and nothing else. Across his boney, bare chest is a tattoo of crossed Rebel flags. He is baring tobacco stained teeth at the camera. One of his hands holds the girl upright by a handful of hair, the other hand is waving a gun.)

Man: You know about Edward Lee? Fangoria says he "pulls no punches."

(The man jerks the girls about. Muffled screams are barely audible.)

Man: Fangoria don't know shit! You know what Edward Lee will do!?!

(The man pulls the girl so she is directly in front of him. He puts the gun to the back of her head and fires. There's a loud BANG and girl's face explodes in a shower of blood, bone, and brains.)

Man: He'll put a bullet through your fuckin' face!

(The corpse slumps to the floor and off camera.)

(*The image changes to a book cover.
"Bullet Through Your Face" by Edward Lee.
The cover image is a close-up painting of
a bullet exiting someone's forehead.*)

Man voiceover: "Bullet Through Your Face,"
out now on Deadite Press. Buy it bitch!

ROUND 3

"Your third challenge is going to be a little different than your first two," said the video girl, "You have shown that you have technical skill on how to handle food but there is more to cooking that just putting ingredients into a pan and then onto a plate."

Another tray lowered down from the ceiling to the center table. This one was even bigger than before but instead of ice cream it was piled high with every type of body part imaginable—arms, eyeball, penises, heads, toes, intestines, kidney stones, and so much more.

"Before you is a selection of some of the finest cured meats the world has to offer," the video girl explained. "Your task this round is to create your own centerpiece—your own work of art—using the cuts we've provided. The piece is meant to be admired and nibbled from for the entire evening. But be quick about it, you only have ten minutes."

The screen turned off and the Supreme Chef assumed his position hovering in the center of the room.

"Round three, *Allez cuisine!*"

The three contestants raced to the table. Amy leaned over the piles of preserved viscera to see what she had to work with. She dug her hands in and shifted the flesh piles around. Something small and white poked through a group of spleens. She pushed them out of the way and grabbed what caught her eye.

A tooth. An adult incisor to be specific.

A tooth . . . Bingo!

That was just the stroke of genius she needed. She dug

back into the pile looking for more teeth. She picked up a head in her search and found a few stray teeth buried beneath it. She paused and looked at the head.

Of course—the mouths.

She rushed back to her kitchenette, took the largest pot she could find, and ran back to the meat pile. She grabbed every head she saw and tossed them into the pot. After gathering up about ten heads she rushed them to her cooking space.

Amy reached into the pot and pulled out one of the heads—a woman, though the curing made it impossible to tell age or race. She placed the head on a cutting board and grabbed a nearby steak knife. She wedged the point of the blade between the gums and the top front teeth. She wiggled the knife and the teeth tore away with little problem. Amy repeated this with all the remaining teeth in the mouth (only eight).

She put down the knife and grabbed a soup spoon. She dug the spoon into the left eye socket, careful not to damage the eye itself. The eyeball started to pop forward and Amy flicked the spoon. It popped out and daggled down the cheek from the optic nerve. She picked the steak knife back up and cradled the eye with the other hand. One quick cut and the eyeball was in her hand neat and pretty. She then repeated the process with the head's right eye.

One head down.

Amy picked up the next head from the pot.

I think I might need more eyeballs.

The buzzers went off and their time was up.

"Time! Now show what you have created," said the Supreme Chef. "Buffo, I'm most intrigued over what you made. Go first."

Buffo spun around from his work station and held up a serving tray displaying his work. He had chosen brains as his material. He'd mashed several together into a paste with which he could mold. From this he made a fairly accurate (material considering) replica of the Lincoln Memorial that was almost three feet tall.

That clown has some weird obsession with the civil war.

"Inspiring and educational," said the Supreme Chef, "and what do you have for us Amy?"

Amy turned to face the Supreme Chef holding out her tray. The Supreme Chef couldn't tell what was on the tray from the distance.

"Come closer," he called.

She stepped forward. On the counter behind her sat a sculpture constructed from a large sternum. The bone was cleaned of any meat and blanched white. Connected to the bottom of the sternum was a skull. Its top was cut off and the insides hollowed out. Its mouth hung wide open. Beneath both these objects was another head on the floor. This one had its skull intact but set up so the hollowed out eye sockets were staring at the ceiling. Its mouth was open as well.

Amy displayed her tray to the Supreme Chef; a simple hors d'oeuvres spread of eyeballs, each with a tooth inserted into the pupil.

Amy held up her free hand, pointing her index finger and indicating for him to watch. She picked up one of the eyes and popped it into her mouth. She chewed all the meat away and swallowed, being careful to keep the tooth in her mouth.

She walked closer to the sternum/head display on the counter. When she was about ten feet away she stopped, stood still for a moment, and then spat out the tooth. The tooth flew through the air and hit the center of the sternum. It bounced down into the opening of the skull and rattled around a few times, then rolled slowly out the open mouth. It fell straight down flew the air into the waiting mouth of the head on the ground.

Amy turned to the Supreme Chef and bowed.

"Marvelous," he said, "just marvelous."

He turned to the last contestant. "Finally, Sliceatron. What did you create?"

The cyborg stepped aside revealing his counter top. All the cyborg had done was grab a torso, two arms, two legs, and a head and assembled them on the countertop in their proper positions.

"*Tsk Tsk,* I expected more," judged the Supreme Chef, "this is amateurish with not even hint of originality. A first year cooking school student would be embarrassed."

"SLICEATRON NOT PROGRAMED TO COMPLETE TASK FOR ROUND," said the cyborg in a jerky static-distorted voice.

"Oh cyber-man, your precision is unrivaled but there is not even a hint of passion or heart," said the Supreme Chef with a touch of pity. "You are an ice cream sundae without the sprinkles. *Torisaru!*"

Red lights and *BBBUUUZZZZZZ* and Sliceatron was gone.

A very thin middle-aged woman pops on the video screen. She has tightly cut short black hair and is wearing a black turtle neck.

The video girl gives a voice over, "Sliceatron is one of the luckiest contestants to ever be eliminated. In conjunction with the Center for Public Art, he is being donated to one of the greatest living artists of our time—Rita Ainsworth!"

The woman on screen starts talking, "I see great potential with this 'metal man' to create a piece that examines the placement of man in this modern, technologically obsessed world. I will fashion his machine parts into a replica of a television, but instead of a screen there will be an automated mechanical jaw. The flesh parts will be preserved and installed on a conveyer belt that will loop in and out of the mouth.

"The piece will be a wake-up call to the world and a dramatic statement on mankind being eternally consumed by its own creations. I have recently been selected as the next artist in residence for the art channel, so starting next Monday on channel 93 at eight p.m. eastern standard time, the whole world will be able to view it 24/7 for two weeks."

Rita Ainsworth disappeared and the video girl appeared on screen. "Thanks! That sounds super!" she squealed. "Now, we're going to take a brief break to give our final two contestants a chance to rest and mentally prepare for their final challenge. But don't worry everyone, we'll be right back."

COMMERCIAL BREAK

(A very skinny man is running down a dark alleyway. He is wearing yellow jeans two sizes too small, a Goonies t-shirt, bright red shoes, a pink scarf, and oversized grandmother sunglasses. He is fleeing in terror from something unknown. His outfit is not designed for a quick getaway and he runs with obvious difficulty.

He stumbles over his own feet and falls into a pile of cardboard boxes filled with trash. The camera zooms in on his terrified face turning around. We can now see that he has an asymmetrical haircut that covers the right side of his face. There is a bright blond streak through the front of his hair.

Image changes to the wall of the alleyway and a large shadow falling across it. We can't tell much but we can make out the silhouette of a man with a shotgun.

Close-up of scared boy)

Emo kid: Who are you? What did I ever do to you?

(View from the perspective of the emo kid looking up. There is a man wearing a black leather jacket with a white t-shirt. His hair is slicked back in a style that would be stylish in the nineteen fifties. He bears more than a passing resemblance to the Fonz. Unlike the Fonz, this guy has a shotgun that is pointed straight at the camera.)

Johnny: I'm Johnny and I'm here to save the day.

(*The shotgun goes off.*)

Quick cut to the interior of a bar. It is a smoky dive with a jukebox blaring Buddy Holly in the background. Johnny is playing pinball. He is no longer wearing the leather jacket but we can now see he has a pack of cigarettes rolled up in his t-shirt's sleeve.

Next to him is a stunningly beautiful woman. She wears black leather pants and a crass tank-top. She has a giant green Mohawk and multiple lip, nose, eyebrow, and ear piercings. She is a sobbing wreck pleading with Johnny.)

Jenny: But Johnny, don't you know I love you? You could leave all this behind and start a life with me.

Johnny: I have to.

Jenny: But why Johnny, why?

Johnny: I . . . I just hate them so much.

(*Image of Johnny standing in the middle of a street, his shotgun slung across his shoulders. He is standing in front of a small art gallery. The sign in the front window is advertising a special exhibit composed of "found art" that promises to be an "eye-opening examination of gender." Without warning the building explodes.*

Johnny gives no indication that anything happened.)

Title cards on top of image: HIPSTER HUNTER BY JEFF BURK

Title cards change: COMING NEXT SUMMER FROM ERASERHEAD PRESS

BUFFO

The room was small, bare, and cold, but Buffo didn't care. Comfort was not a concern for him—that was for those less enlightened.

He sat cross-legged in the lotus position. Both his hands were held out, palm up, in front of his body. In one sat a seltzer bottle, in the other a hand-buzzer—these were his offerings to the clown Gods of fun and surprising flavors.

His mind focused on the red ball that sat on his nose. He concentrated and imagined all of his energy being encompassed by that ball as he extended his consciousness to make connection with universal flavor.

The boundaries of his body slipped away (as his sect symbolized with face paint) and his mind whirled.

Buzzing alarms and red lights flashed around Buffo, signaling the beginning of the fourth and final round. He opened his eyes, pocketed the seltzer bottle and hand-buzzer, and got to his feet.

He grabbed his fake nose and squeezes it twice, saying "honk" each time.

Buffo was ready for battle.

AMY

Amy took off her jeans in the center of the room. She sat down and the floor was cold on her ass but she didn't even pause. There were only a few minutes before the commercials were over.

She placed both of her hands on her left thigh and pushed down. There was a clicking sound and the hidden door on her leg sprung open. It was a small compartment, hidden from even the most invasive search, containing a glass vial of clear liquid.

Amy shut the door on her leg and quickly got dressed. She examined the container she just produced. Her mind flashed back to when she was a small girl and her grandmother, being her only living family, had the surgery on to her.

Her grand ma-ma had placed the vial into her leg. "One day you will need this. I have read your cupcake crumbs and the future is already decided—you will regain what was stolen from us long ago."

"But what's that grand ma-ma?" said little Amy, looking with wonder at the object being carefully placed inside her.

"A gift my grand ma-ma gave to me—the secret to ultimate flavor," said grand ma-ma. "Never take it out. Never mention it to anybody. Not until the moment is right."

"How will I know when it is right?"

Red lights and buzzing tore Amy out of her memories. She palmed the vial. Her grand ma-ma's response lingered in her head.

"You'll know."

ROUND 4

"Alright, you did it," squealed the video girl. She now had a noise-maker and a plastic party hat. She blew into the noise maker and then continued, "you made it to the final round! This is it, the end of the show. One of you will be assuming the head chef position at any restaurant, anywhere in the world. The other one of you . . . won't. Gomenasai!

"You have proven that you know how to select meat, serve a dish, and understand the art of presentation. Now you will answer the most important question—can you cook? You will complete against each other in a cook-off. We are supplying a secret ingredient that your dish must be based around. You will each have half an hour to prepare and then the Supreme Chef will sample your creations and decide a winner.

"And without further ado, this week's secret ingredient is . . . bacon!"

A massive circular tray of raw bacon lowered down from the ceiling to the table in the center of the area. It was at least ten feet across and the pile of sliced meat was at least a meter high. Amy had never dreamed of so much bacon in one spot at one time. She immediately started salivating.

"We are supplying the finest bacon humanly possible— cut from the finest cattle, fresh from the fattie farms in Hyōgo Prefecture. You are permitted to use the bacon in any way you wish, but the basis of your dish must be bacon.

"Under the counters in your kitchenettes you will find a Replicat 7300—the finest in replication technology. The machine will link with your mind and produce any other ingredient you may need for your dishes. The only limit is your imagination.

"I hope you're ready."

The screen darkened and the Supreme Chef flew to his standard spot in the middle of the room. "Final round, *Allez cuisine!*"

Amy and Buffo rushed to the bacon. Neither bothered with utensils or plates of any kind. They both just reached in, grabbed handfuls of the greasy meat (Amy only grabbed one handful, the other hand still hid the vial), and ran back to their kitchenettes.

Amy grabbed a pan, put it on the stove, threw some bacon in, and set the heat.

She kneeled down to use the Replicat 7300, a black box about twice the size of a normal microwave. It had a door on the front, just like a microwave, but no buttons to push. Amy had heard of these machines but she had never had the opportunity to use one.

Let's try this out. Milk.

She opened the door and inside was a container of milk. She took it out and unscrewed the top. She quickly glanced around to confirm that what she was doing was out of sight of the hidden cameras, the Supreme Chef, and Buffo.

The top of the vial popped easily off and the contents quickly deposited into the milk. Once the container was empty it disappeared in Amy's hand. It didn't melt away or turn to dust, simply one minute it was there and the next it was not.

She stood up and placed the milk on the counter. She did another quick scan of the room to make sure she got away with it. . . whatever it was she just did. *What was in that vial?*

The guards made no indication they saw anything. The Supreme Chef sat on his throne just staring off into space. Buffo was . . . Buffo was staring directly at her. His eyes glared and he no longer looked like the peaceful clown cook in touch with the universe like before—he looked outraged.

Did he see? He couldn't have.

It was too late. The deed had already been done. There was nothing more Amy could do but continue cooking for the final showdown. The clock was ticking.

The buzzers went off ending the final round. The Supreme Chef floated down and landed his throne on top of the mound of bacon.

"Time," he boomed.

Amy and Buffo brought up their dishes to be judged.

"Buffo," said the Supreme Chef, "you shall be first. What do you have for me?"

Buffo was carrying several balloons that floated about him. Each balloon had about a dozen brown globs sticking to it. The globs looked like small pieces of fried bread. Buffo held out one of the balloons.

The Supreme Chef took it, "and what is this you have here?"

Buffo held out one of his hands, spread his fingers and turned the hand around demonstrating it was empty, snapped his fingers, and magically produced a white card. He handed the card over.

"Bacon Balloon Polyps," read the Supreme Chef.

He examined the balloon, removed one of the "polyps"

and popped it into his mouth. He chewed and smiled, "Delicious."

"And what do you, Amy, have for me?" he asked turning to Amy.

She offered up the large cold glass, "Bacon and Berry Smoothie."

He grabbed the glass with his free hand and took a sip. "Amazing."

Amy watched, trying not to betray her nervousness. She had no idea what was in that vial that she dumped into the smoothie that now the one and only Supreme Chef was drinking.

The truth, dear reader, will be disappointing to you but would be wondrous to Amy, Buffo, and the Supreme Chef. The vial contained nothing more than a concentrated solution of monosodium glutamate, better known as MSG. Ancient health codes had long ago rid the world of the flavor enhancing miracle known as MSG but, as fate would have it, Amy had come into possession of the very last drops.

The Supreme Chef looked back and forth at the bacon balloon polyps and the bacon and berry smoothie.

"Silence, while I consider these treats," said the Supreme Chef as he shut his eyes to concentrate.

Hey kids, who will the Supreme Chef choose as the winner? Play along at home and decide your own winner!

Buffo's Bacon Balloon Polyps

1 lb bacon, cooked until crisp, drained on paper towels
2 (8 ounce) packages cream cheese, softened
1/2 cup Miracle Whip
1/2 cup shredded parmesan cheese
1 cup shredded sharp cheddar cheese
1/8 teaspoon garlic powder
1/8 teaspoon onion powder
1/2 teaspoon Worcestershire sauce

Process the bacon in a food processor. In a large bowl, beat cream cheese and Miracle Whip until well mixed. Beat in the remaining ingredients (except the bacon). Beat in the bacon only until mixed. Shape into small balls and stick on a balloon or wrap in plastic wrap. Chill.

Amy's Bacon and Berry Smoothie:

1/2 cup yogurt
1 cup milk
1/4 cup bacon grease
1/2 cup frozen raspberries and blueberries
1 teaspoon bacon bits
4 strips of bacon
1-2 tablespoon dark chocolate powder
1 Vial essence of flavor (500 milligrams of MSG or a generous dosage of LSD is an appropriate substitute)

Blend all ingredients. Drink daily. Die at 38.

The Supreme Chef opened his eyes, "Amy Kaga, I declare you the winner!"

Amy's heart leapt in her chest.

"What!" screamed Buffo. Both the Supreme Chef and Amy turned to him in shock.

"She cheated, I saw her put something in her dish. Something she brought in with her."

"Why didn't you say something earlier?" asked the Supreme Chef.

"Because I was sure my skill could best any dirty trick she had," Buffo glared at Amy, "but her bad mojo is very strong indeed."

The Supreme Chef turned to Amy. "Is this true?"

She looked up at him and met his eyes. "No."

He looked at her for a few moments and then down at the glass of bacon and berry smoothie. He held up the glass and inspected it, sniffed the drink carefully, and took another long, slow slip. The Supreme Chef smacked his lips and sat silent.

He turned to Buffo. "Do you have any proof?"

"She had some kind of vial," said Buffo, "but it disappeared after she emptied it . . ."

"Due to lack of evidence, I must decide in Amy Kaga's favor," ruled the Supreme Chef. "To make such an accusation and have no evidence brings grave dishonor to you and your clan, Buffo. I have no other choice than to doom you to the greatest punishment someone of your obvious talent could ever know—a lifetime of fast food service!"

The Supreme Chef pointed dramatically at Buffo as the clown screamed, "But she cheated!"

There was a bright flash and the clown was gone.

The video screen turned on showing Buffo standing beside a deep fryer holding a basket of French Fries. A pimply teen wearing a paper hat walked up to him and started yelling. The footage had no audio but Buffo's makeup made his streaming tears abundantly clear.

"Oh, poor Buffo."

The image changed to the video girl.

"Congratulations Amy Kaga, you have cooked for your life. You are today's champion and, after a quick commercial break, we'll join you in the Winner's Circle for your reward!"

COMMERCIAL BREAK

(*The screen shows a young girl of about ten. She looks nervous as an arm from off-screen offers her a pack of cigarettes.*

Off-screen female voice, obviously belonging to someone older than the girl we can see: Go ahead, just try. One won't hurt you.

The girl takes a cigarette and nervously holds it up to her lips while another hand quickly appears from off-screen with a lighter.

Screen changes to an old woman in a hospital bed hooked up to a respirator. The heart monitor she's hooked up to flat lines.

Screen changes to a young man in his twenties walking through a forest. He is wearing a backpack and hiking boots. He has a broad smile as he takes in nature.

Camera zooms in on a small pile of sticks in his path that he is unaware of.

The man trips over the sticks and falls off the path. The camera zooms back revealing that he was walking next to a very large, steep hill. He rolls down the hill hitting sharp rocks, tree stumps, and thorn bushes. The viewer can hear loud cracks as his bones snap against the obstacles. After a good thirty seconds of this his body finally comes to a stop at the bottom. Then a black bear leaps on him from off camera and starts eating.

Screen changes to two middle-age non-descript men leaning in and kissing.

Image flashes to the Earth exploding.)

The screen goes black and "FAGS KILL" flashes up in white letters.

Then: HOMOBOMB BY JEFF BURK

WINNER'S CIRCLE

Amy stepped into the large circular room that everyone knew from TV but few had ever stepped into. The room was only about fifty feet across but the ceiling went hundreds of feet into the air. Great glass columns lined the edges of the room extending from floor to ceiling. In the center of the room the Supreme Chef sat on his throne.

"Approach," he said.

Amy did and got down on one knee, as was the custom for winners on the show.

"Amy Kaga, you have proven yourself. You have bested your challengers and have earned the honor to serve others. Tell me, what kitchen in the world do you desire?"

"My great-great-grandmother was a grand-master chef back in the old country," began Amy, "she was a simple woman, born to a poor family, and married to a poor blacksmith. The two weathered great difficulty in their life but they were happy. The highlight of their life was the one child they had—a girl, my great-grandmother.

"Her mother taught her the family secrets of cooking and her father taught her the art of forging steel. Combing the two she created a new school of cooking—Wu-Fu. Have you heard of it?"

The Supreme Chef arched one eyebrow but didn't otherwise respond.

Amy sneered. "Yeah you have. Wu-Fu is not just a legend. It gave birth to all the great schools of cooking— Way of the Simmer, the Blackened Path, even the Clown School of Cooking has its origins in Wu-Fu.

"Most famously, my great-grandmother forged special instruments of cooking. Her skill at crafting the perfect pot, pan, or knife was unmatched. She spent the last twenty years of her life working on one utensil—the perfect knife was what she called it.

"One day, after all that time of toiling, she finally finished. While taking her prize home to show her friends and family she was mugged by a common thief. He managed to wrestle the sword from her and stabbed her with her very creation. He left her to bleed out in the street.

"My family considered the treasure lost but I learned that the thief sold the blade to a private collector who in turn sold it to a television studio—he even made up a silly story about the holder being the greatest chef in the world and master of all flavor.

"My great grandmother made that sword—the Blade-O-Matic 5600," Amy pointed at the weapon that hung from the Supreme Chef's waist.

"What kitchen do you desire?" the Supreme Chef repeated.

"I desire the "Cook for Your Life's kitchen."

He nodded. His eyes stayed hard but a slight smile betrayed the corner of his lips. "I knew one day you would come."

He stood and drew the sword from his belt. He sliced through the air twice and spun the weapon around, handing it to Amy hilt first.

She took the sword and marveled at its beauty.

After so many generations the Blade-O-Matic 5600 was finally returned to its makers.

The Supreme Chef kneeled before Amy and lowered his head. He mumbled a prayer to the Gods of graters, steamers, and nonstick pans.

Amy unsheathed the sword and pressed the flat side of the blade against her forehead. She closed her eyes and said a short prayer to her ancestors.

With no warning, she swung the blade down and lopped off the Supreme Chef's head. The head hit the ground, bounced once, and then rolled a few feet away from the throne. The body crashed to the floor instantly.

Amy kneeled down next to the corpse and carefully removed his cape. Beneath the regal covering, the Supreme Chef wore a plain white chef's uniform. She wrapped the cape around herself and sheathed the sword at her side. She was now the new Supreme Chef and she sat down in her rightful floating throne.

(*Amy shifts about in the chair getting use to the seat. She adjusts the collar of the robe and then stares straight into the camera.*)

Amy: "Ladies and Gentlemen, you have been watching "Cook for Your Life!" Join us next week for another tasty episode. Goodnight."

FADE OUT

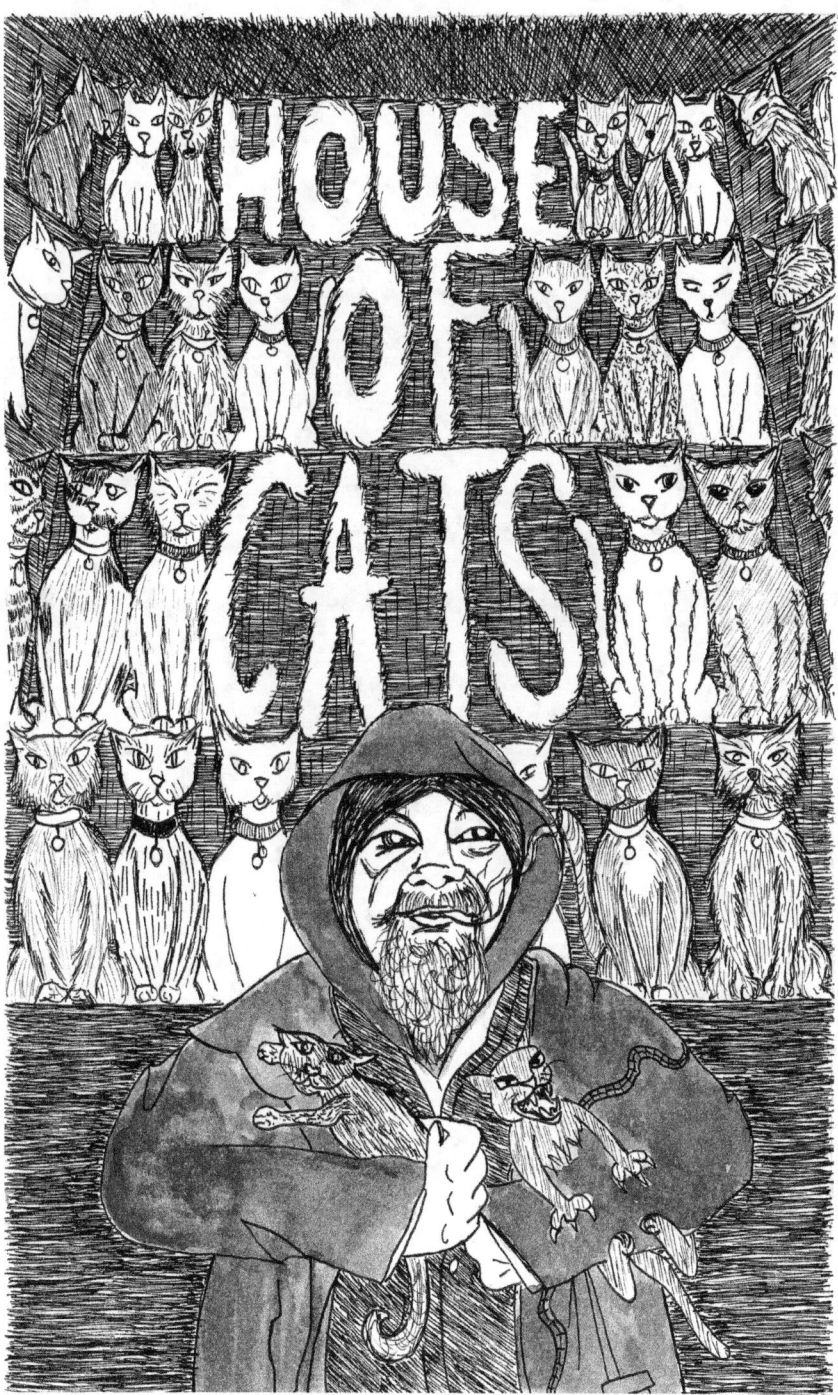

Once upon a time, in a strange land know as Portland, Oregon, there lived a man who went by the name Jasper. No last name, just Jasper.

Jasper liked to tell people that he called the entire city "home," which was a nice way of explaining that he was homeless.

Jasper spent his days pushing his grocery cart around the city collecting cans to turn in at the recycling center. Sometimes he would just sit outside one of the city's tourist hotspots and panhandle.

He spent his nights beneath one of the city's many bridges. There he would eat whatever food he was able to pull out of a dumpster and drink cheap beer, bought with either his recycling or panhandling money, until he blacked out.

Most mornings he woke up wet. Portland is a very rainy city and unless you have a roof, and a real one—cardboard shacks just don't hold up—you wake up wet most mornings.

Jasper was reflecting upon this terribly irksome fact about his lifestyle one afternoon when he stumbled upon a solution.

He had been tin can hunting in the southeast part of the city. He was pushing his stolen shopping cart that contained all his finds from the day's ventures. Enough tin to surely get a six pack of PBR.

The area is a manicured, well-kept residential part of town, the residents mostly yuppies and college-aged-hippies. The people who live there feel safe enough to walk by themselves after dark, get blind drunk with people they never met before, and, most relevant to this story, let their cats roam freely all hours of the day and night.

One of these very cats, a white long-hair, darted beneath Jasper's feet from seemingly nowhere. Jasper stumbled but quickly regained his balance.

The fluffy beast darted again at his feet. Jasper's hands shot down and snatched up the cat. He held it out and looked the animal over.

"RAAAOOOWWW!" it protested and wiggled.

Jasper turned it around, flipped it upside down, and then held it over his head.

"Yeah . . ." he said to himself while tucking the cat under his left arm.

". . . raow." said the cat.

He rooted around the many pockets in his old and dirty leather over-coat and found the ball of twine he always kept on him. With a few quick flicks of his wrist, the cat was bound. Its legs pressed tight against its body by the twine wrapped around it like a package.

"Raow?"

Jasper placed the cat in his shopping-cart and continued on his way, keeping his eyes open for more cats to catch. The next five were easy, there were so many cats in this city that by shear probability, he was bound to run into a few friendly, slow, or fat ones.

But he needed some way to catch the number of cats he required for his plan. He looked down at his five prisoners and they looked back up at him—hate burning in their eyes.

What do cats like? How can I bring them to me and make them happy they did it?

It suddenly clicked with him and he went to the nearest pet store. The clerk on duty was either really stoned or astonishingly apathetic because she didn't bat one heavily mascaraed eye as Jasper pushed his shopping cart, complete with five kitty hostages, through the store and the check-out.

Once he got outside, he opened up the plastic store bag and pulled out three one-pound bags of the finest ground catnip he could buy. He put two bags in the pockets of his coat and he tore open the third bag. The sudden wafting aroma of catnip made the cats in the cart cry out louder.

Jasper dumped half the contents of the bag over the shopping cart and everything within. He poured the rest of the bag over himself, taking care to rub it into his clothes and hair. The cats in the cart purred loudly as they entered a drug-induced bliss.

Jasper pushed the cart back to the cat-infested neighborhood and, in almost no time at all, cats were coming to him. He just had to pick them up, tie them, and put them in the cart. If he rubbed some catnip on their faces, they put up no fight at all. *I must have gotten some primo shit*, he thought.

Soon his shopping cart was filled to the brim with purring and mewing drugged-up and tied up cats.

He pushed his cart back to his normal spot under the bridge. It was a desolate spot, a fifty yard by fifty yard grass clearing, bordered by highways and long-abandoned warehouses. A private location where he felt safe sleeping and leaving what meager belongings he had behind when he went out.

Jasper took the cats out of the cart and piled them on the ground. He lined them up in rows, all facing the same direction, and began to tie the cats together, making cat-boards. Then he stacked the cat-boards on top of each other, tied them together, and created a cat-wall.

But then Jasper was out of cats. It was obvious he was going to need *a lot* of cats to complete this project.

He picked up the cat-wall. It hissed at him and its collective predicament. He carried it over to a tree near the edge of the clearing. He leaned the cat-wall against the tree, and then tied it in place.

"Behold," Jasper said, stepping back and holding out his arms in awe, "my house of cats."

The first night it really wasn't a cat-house, it was more of a cat-lean-to. He slept beneath the cats, and while they did protect him from early morning rain, their incessant mewing made falling asleep almost impossible. It was nice having his head protected, but he really wanted walls.

He got up at the first crack of sunrise and cooked up a hearty breakfast of baked beans. He thought about the coming day. He got a decent haul of cats yesterday, but he needed many more to finish his project. It was going to be a busy day.

"RRRRAAAOOOORRRR!!!"

"You must be hungry," said Jasper. He walked over to the cat-wall, the pot of beans in one hand and a spoon in the other. He dipped the spoon into the pot and scooped out a heap of beans. He held the spoon out to the gray short-haired cat in the second to top row. Its little mouth eagerly gobbled up beans. Jasper moved the spoon on to the next cat in the row. He continued to do this, occasionally having to spoon out more beans, until every cat on the wall was fed.

Once he had finally fed himself, he took his empty cart out into the city and caught cats until it was filled. He did this again and again and again until he completed six trips, the sun was beginning to set, and his clearing was filled with bound, doped-up cats.

Jasper sat down on the ground, exhausted, and pulled a stepped-on cigarette out of his pocket. It was a little bent and smooshed but it was still plenty smokeable.

While he enjoyed his break, Smut and Willy came walking by. Smut was a squat little round man who earn his nick-name for the child porn ring he use to run; its failing was the reason he was out on the streets. Willy was a tall, lanky man who was missing most of his teeth and had a face dotted with open meth sores.

"What's this you've got goin' here?" asked Smut while looking around at all the cats. "You gettin' into the butcher business."

Willy smacked his hands together and slobber rolled down his chin.

"Oh boy, oh boy. It's been so long since I've had me some good Bar-B-Q pussy. We'll take three," Willy said, holding out his left hand with four fingers up.

"These cats ain't for sale," said Jasper.

"Well what then are you going to do with all this livestock?" asked Smut.

"I'm going to live in them," answered Jasper while he took a drag on his smoke.

Smut and Willy shared a look of pure confusion.

Smut pulled Willy close to whisper in his ear. "It appears our dear friend Jasper has finally lost it. The stress of the modern world has simply become too much for him. Let us go on our way and leave this poor boy to his fate."

Willy nodded and they walked away.

Jasper paid their exit no mind. A whirl of angles, figures, and blueprints preoccupied him. He finished his cigarette and stood up. He looked around at all the cats—there had to be over three hundred of them.

He brushed some dirt off his pants and went to work.

Jasper worked all through the night and all through the next day and even the night after that. As the first rays of morning light broke on his second day of work, he was finished.

Standing fifteen feet wide by twenty feet long and a dozen feet high, it was just one room but it wasn't bad. Not bad at all for one man and a bunch of cats.

The house was a simple four walls and a roof design. All the cats faced toward the interior, to make them easier to feed and to keep their wastes on the outside of his home.

Jasper walked around the house. Hundreds of tails flicked along the outside, making the house look like some strange furry-tentacle monster.

He walked up to the back of the house, braced his hands on the "wall," and gave a hard shake. Outside of an angry mew from inside, nothing happened. The building stood firm.

He walked back to the front and opened up the door. The door was his proudest innovation for the house. It's not easy to make hinges from cats, but he found a way.

Jasper entered the house and shut the door. At once, hundreds of tiny heads turned to face him. Scores of glowing, sharp eyes stared and wondered what he was going to do next. He smiled back at them.

"Don't worry kitties, I'm not going to hurt you. Welcome to your new home."

At first it was difficult getting used to the new living situation, for both Jasper and the cats.

Jasper had to work a lot harder to get enough food to feed all the new mouths. It took a lot more cans, or hunting out dumpsters in far flung parts of the city. Sometimes Jasper even went to bed hungry, just so the cat-house was fed.

God forbid if he didn't get enough food. The first cat that wasn't fed would start mewing and then all the other cats would pick up the cry. Soon it would be so loud inside the house that Jasper couldn't have a clear thought.

But as time went on, he got better at getting food and after a few weeks the routine was normal for him. As he and his home were better fed, they both were happier. Once a week, Jasper had to shovel all the shit away from the sides of his house.

It was a lot of work taking care of the cat-house but Jasper didn't care. He finally had something that was his. Something that he made. Something that was truly his own.

As time went on, the cats in the house became closer, beyond just their bonds. Before, one cat would mew and the rest joined in, but now they mewed together. Three hundred cats with one brain and one voice

When winter came, Jasper couldn't have been happier that he put all that effort into building the cat-house. Their body heat kept the inside nice and toasty. Jasper even noticed the cats seemed to like being bound together. They snuggled extra tight together so that the interior of the house actually got smaller, their eyes drooped and, in unison, they snored.

By the end of the winter the cats were so used to their new situation that they forgot all about past families and friends. There was just them and Jasper, and Jasper felt the same way.

As spring came, the clearing bloomed with purple wild flowers. Every night he lay in his dirty, dumpstered mattress and fell asleep as the purring of his house filled his senses.

Then came the fateful day that was the end of his happiness.

Jasper awoke one morning and before he could rub the sleep out of his eyes, he knew something was wrong. The cats were quietly growling. Their eyes darted about as if looking for some danger they knew was there but could not find. Their little bodies vibrated from frustration and rage.

Jasper sprung from his bed and threw on some mud stained clothes. He tried talking sweetly and telling the cats they were "pretty kitties" but his house would not be calmed.

He went out the front door and his entire body was swatted by a swarm of angrily whipping tales. He stumbled forward, temporarily blinded by all the fur and fell to his knees. Regaining his composure, he looked around. He immediately saw what was upsetting his house.

On the other side of the lot, where last night a pleasant plot of wildflowers grew, was a house made of dogs. Hundreds of dogs. All shapes and sizes. Tied together, facing toward the interior, a building almost twice the size of his own.

The door to the dog-house opened and out stepped a man fat enough to be in a circus sideshow. His T-shirt, stretched to nearly tearing at the seams, read "I Fuck on the First Date." The beef-sides he had for legs were covered in dirty and torn light blue sweat-pants.

As he left his house, all the dogs started barking at once. Jasper's cat-house screeched and shook so hard it almost moved.

"Shut up!" yelled the fat-man at his house, "Shut up, you fuckin' mutts."

The dog-house quieted down.

The fat-man waddled over to Jasper and grabbed Jasper's right hand. The fat-man, who stood at least three feet taller than him, effortlessly hoisted Jasper to his feet while shaking his hand vigorously at the same time.

"Well good mornin' to yah," boomed the fat-man, "you must be my new neighbor. Pleased to meet yah, I's Herbert."

"Did you build that last night?" Jasper pointed at the dog-house. "I've been squatting here for years. My house has been here for months. This is my home. You can't just move in like this."

Herbert rubbed his acne-ridden chin. "Is that so . . ."

Jasper waited for a response but none came.

"That's so," said Jasper, exasperated. "This is my spot. I've was here first and your house is upsetting my house."

"Yeeeeeaaaaaahhhh, I'll tell yah what," said Herbert while slapping Jasper on the back so hard that it nearly took his breath away. "This is a big spot and I'm just going stay."

91

He waddled away from Jasper and when he got to his door he turned back around. "We'll show 'em that dogs and cats can live togetha." He chuckled to himself and then went inside his house and shut the door.

Jasper turned back to his house, its tails still twitching angrily, and went back inside.

All the heads turned to him, their eyes all asking the same question—*did you fix it? Did you make things better?*

"I'm sorry kitties," said Jasper, "I'm . . . I'm not sure what we should do."

He didn't see an immediate solution to his problem. Using force to make Herbert and his house of dogs leave wasn't an option. He'd destroy Jasper in a fight.

So Jasper decided to try and live with this new inconvenience. But his house was not happy with this course of action. Whenever the dogs barked, his house would start violently shaking with a cacophony of pissed off mews.

The rest of the time, the cats silently seethed. They never seemed hungry anymore. Jasper had a hard time getting them to eat. After a few days, Jasper was sure his house was shrinking—the cats were getting thinner.

Jasper stopped sleeping. In addition to the constant atmosphere of anger his house gave off, Herbert snored loud enough to disturb Jasper all night every night. Every few hours the dog-house started barking which then set off the cat-house. Herbert always seemed to sleep through that.

After a full week, Jasper decided enough was enough. The sun came up and Jasper got out of bed from another sleepless night, put on clothes, and went straight out his door to Herbert's. Jasper banged on the door, each knock punctuated by a yelp from inside.

Herbert opened the door and stared down at Jasper.

"Wadda yah want?"

"This just cannot go on," said Jasper. "I was here first. This is my land. I must ask you to leave. You presence and your house are making my life unbearable. So, now go, before I am forced to do something drastic."

Herbert stared down at Jasper. His face did not betray

any kind of emotion.

"Fuck off," he said and then slammed the door. The door-dogs yelped.

Jasper stood there for a moment, staring at the door. Not sure what to do.

He turned around and walked back into his cat-house.

Knock. Rawr! Knock. Rawr! Knock. Rawr!

Jasper opened up his door and a thin, balding man in a suit stood on the other side. He held a clipboard and he jotted down notes while looking over the house.

He went *tsk, tsk, tsk* under his breath.

He looked at Jasper. "Good day sir. Are you a mister," he paused and consulted his clipboard, "Jasper?"

"I am."

"I'm from the city and I'm here to inform you that you did not get the proper permits to construct a structure of this nature within city limits."

Jasper didn't know what the man was talking about. "'Structure of this nature'? You mean, cats?"

The man ignored Jasper and continued. "Now that I'm seeing this first hand, it is obvious that there is no way to bring this building up to code."

The man wrote something down on the clipboard and then quickly tore off a piece of paper and handed it to Jasper.

"I'm sorry to inform you this," explained the man, "but you have exactly thirty days to vacate your property before the city declares it condemned and it is leveled."

"Thirty days? What am I suppose to do? I can't take this apart. I tried the other day to do that, just to get away from that jerk." Jasper pointed across the clearing at Herbert's house and was surprised, though he really shouldn't have been, to see Herbert standing in his doorway watching the interaction.

The man speaking snapped back Jasper's attention. "Not my problem. You have been given your thirty day notice."

"What if I don't leave?"

"Then you'll be bulldozed with your shack."

Jasper pointed at Herbert's. "What about him? You tearing down his place too?"

"No."

"Why not?"

"He filled out the correct forms."

"But his house is made of dogs, mine is made of cats. What's the difference?"

"He filled out the correct forms."

"Come on-"

"Sir, I must bid you a good day," the man nodded at Jasper. "You have been given your notice." And with that, he quickly turned and went speeding off.

Jasper just stared blankly, not knowing what to do. He was going to lose his home. Not just lose it—they were going to destroy it.

"Tough break neighbor," yelled Herbert. Then he laughed and shut his door.

Jasper stepped into Papa Scorpion's hut. The small shack, assembled from stolen road signs, was way out on the eastern outskirts of the city, far beyond where any derelict normally wandered—unless they were looking for the services of Papa Scorpion.

The small frail old man gestured for Jasper to follow. Papa Scorpion was dressed in clothes that were little more than rags with a bright red Members Only jacket over-top. It was hard to believe someone so weak-looking held so much power.

Jasper looked around the inside of the shack. Books, papers, and jars littered two tables and a ratty bed. The inside walls were plastered with nothing but CAUTION signs and those signs that warn of electrical shocks that have the little guy getting blasted with the lightning bolt.

Papa Scorpion took notice of what Jasper was looking at. "It's best to heed their warning." He wheezed out a laugh and immediately started coughing and gasping

He took an inhaler out of a jacket pocket, took a puff, and regained control of his breathing. "Now what can Papa

Scorpion do for you?"

"I want to take vengeance," said Jasper, "on a man I hate."

Papa Scorpion nodded and looked at Jasper. He regarded him for a moment and then smiled. "I know you. You're the crazy guy with the house of cats."

"And you're someone who calls himself Papa Scorpion."

Papa Scorpion laughed. "You got me there." He turned serious very quickly. "I can do want you want."

He went back to a pile of junk and rooted around, pushing aside papers, books, and various crap. He then turned around and held out a glass vial to Jasper.

Jasper took it and held up the vial, looking into it. It contained a small amount of clear liquid that looked, and moved, just like water.

"Oderless, colorless, and tasteless," explained Papa Scorpion. "Just that small amount will doom a strong man to death."

Jasper continued to look into the vial and thought of Herbert's immense size. "I think I'm going to need a lot more."

Knock. Arf! Knock. Arf! Knock. Arf!

Herbert opened the door and stared down at Jasper. "What do yah want?"

Jasper held up his hands in mock defense. "No need for aggression. I'm here to make peace. As you know, tomorrow I must leave. I thought on my last night here, we might actually have a good time."

Herbert eyed Jasper with suspicion.

"I got Bar-B-Q ribs and beer."

Jasper stepped aside and called attention to a steel folding table that was in between their two houses. It was covered with beef ribs dripping with sauce.

Herbert didn't need to hear anymore. He pushed Jasper aside and moved quicker than he had in years to the table. He immediately grabbed hunks of meat and bone and shoveled them into his mouth.

"I'll be back out with the beer," said Jasper as he stepped inside his house. He emerged with two large glass steins of beer. As he took a seat he passed Herbert a glass.

Herbert wasn't the smartest of people, but he was smart enough not to take a drink he didn't see poured. Especially not from someone who may hate him.

Herbert made like he was going to take a sip but right before the stein touched his lips, he quickly set it down. "Ah love what yah did wit yah house. Lak the ruff," he said pointing.

Jasper turned to look at his house of cats. "Thank you, I put a lot of hard work into it. I'll be sad to leave."

While Jasper had turned his head, Herbert slyly switched their glasses. *That'll teach 'im*, thought Herbert.

Jasper turned back to Herbert. "But enough of that sad talk. Let's eat and drink."

"Cheers," said Herbert holding up his drink.

And that's what they did. They ate and drank well into the morning hours. For each refill of their steins, Jasper went inside his house. Each time he came out, Herbert would trick him in some way and switch their glasses.

As the hour grew late and the sun was threatening to break, they decided to call it a night.

"Yah know, yah not so bad," drunkenly slurred Herbert while he hugged Jasper goodnight.

That little shit doesn't know I was switching the steins all night, thought Herbert, *I ain't stupid. He ain't poisoning me.*

Herbert chuckled to himself on the way inside his home and promptly passed out on his bad.

Jasper entered his cat-house, where there was nothing. He always had small trinkets around along with the many things he found or stole that he intended to resell. But not anymore. He had gotten rid of everything he could to raise enough money for the food, beer, and, of course, Papa Scorpion's poison.

The same poison that was in every glass both men drank that night.

Fucking bastards. I ain't never ever leaving my home,

thought Jasper, *This is all I ever had and no one's taking that away from me. Not the city and especially not that fat fuck.*

Jasper chuckled as his lungs began to shutdown.

In the house of dogs, Herbert thrashed around on his bed while white foam poured out of his mouth and blood welled of out his eye-sockets.

The cats and dogs joined each other in a howl of mourning for their dying masters.

By the time the sun rose, both men were dead.

The demolition crew never came that day. They were supposed to but they never showed. Nor did they come the day after that. The houses were left by themselves, with their masters dead inside.

Soon the mourning turned to hunger. The houses had not been fed in days.

The house of cats was the first to break. They could smell Jasper's flesh rotting in the center of them all and their eyes had no choice but to look straight at the meat. The hundreds of starving cats wiggled as one toward the body, their restraints slackening around their malnourished bodies. The house imploded and the cats tumbled toward Jasper.

The cats had been bound for so long that they had forgotten how to use their legs. Some lucky ones fell onto the corpse and they immediately began to feast. Their tiny mouths tearing into the soft, just beginning to rot, flesh. The other cats wiggled over the ground, and each other, toward the body.

The ravenous cats quickly consumed the corpse but it didn't satisfy them. The combination of Jasper's death and hunger had snapped the felines' collective mind. They only had one thought. One directive.

Feed.

They turned on each other, consuming every speck of flesh, bone, and fur, eating each other while they themselves were being eaten.

The sounds of the feeding frenzy incensed the dogs.

Each dog shook with a collective desire.

Food.

The house of dogs collapsed inwards and the dogs made short work of Herbert's bloated mass. Then, they too, turned on each other. Their vicious jaws tearing skin and muscle easily away from any neighboring dog.

The two masses of teeth, blood, and hunger tore and feasted at themselves. They thrashed, writhed, and swallowed until there was not one cat or dog left. The clearing, once wild flowers and grass, was just a wet puddle of blood, viscera, and clumps of fur.

Eventually the ground soaked it up and that too was gone.

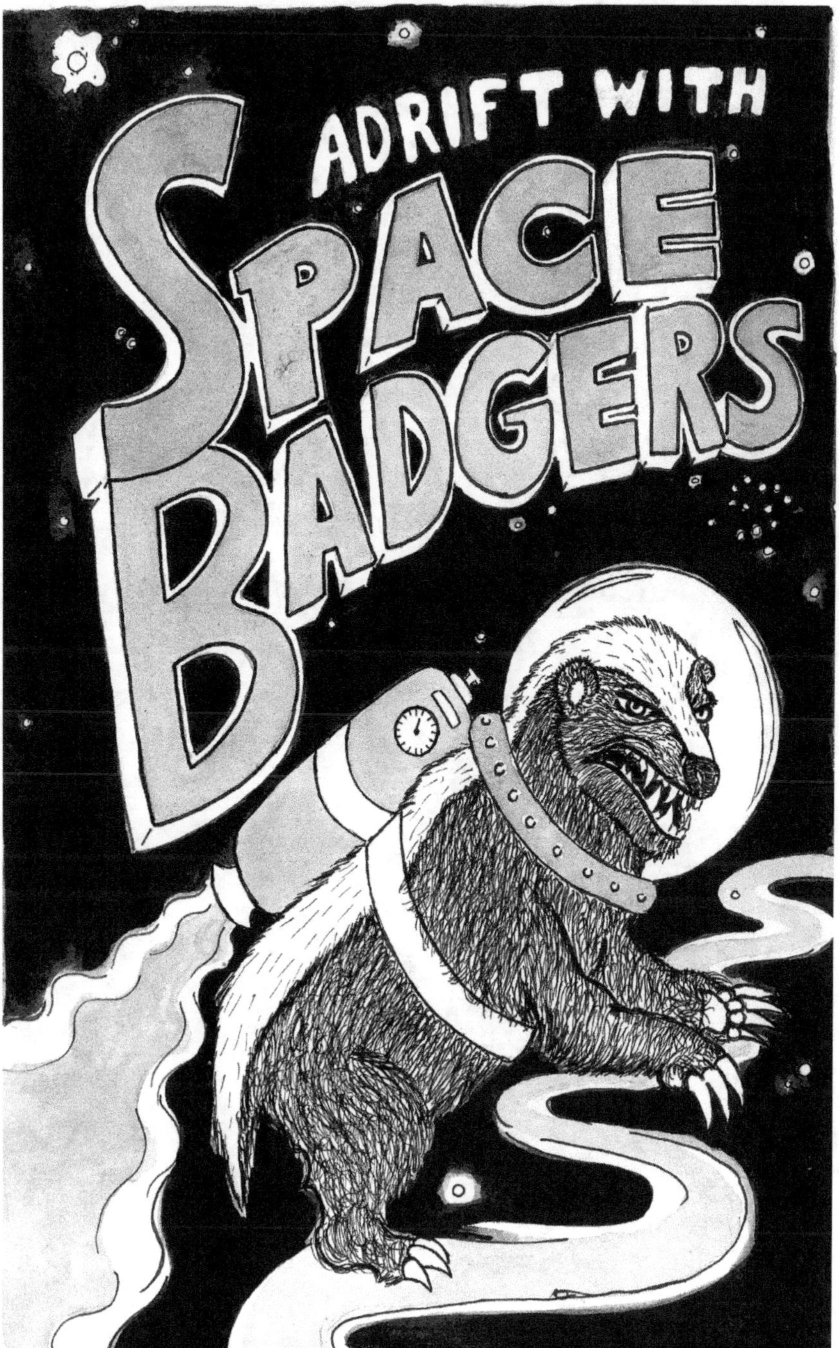
ADRIFT WITH
SPACE
BADGERS

The men, drunk on boredom, blood lust, and bathtub wine, cheered on the two combatants in the center of the ship's hangar.

Most planet-dwellers have heard of space badgers, but have never seen one in real life. They're nasty little buggers. They have claws, sharp teeth and are completely fearless. They look very much like Earth's honey-badger, but wear tanks of air on their backs. A hose connects each tank to a clear, glass, fish-bowl helmet covering the badger's head. These pieces look like equipment, but they are actually part of the space badger's body. The species evolved these appendages to survive in both the vacuum of space and in pressurized environments. Darwin never saw these little bitches coming.

Whereas sailors have to deal with rats stowing aboard ships—spacemen have to deal with space badgers. The feisty little creatures build nests inside of machinery and fuck up the workings of all sorts of internal systems if they're not immediately dealt with. Nothing is more annoying than to suddenly lose main power for a day or two and be stuck dead in space just because you've got a family of space badgers getting all cozy in the reactors.

Therefore, most people who work in space have no patience or sympathy for the little fuckers. It's considered standard practice to kill all space badgers on sight. Or if you don't kill them right away, you catch them and keep them for space badger fights.

Like the one the maintenance crew was watching.

They gathered around a barrel full of water, placing bets on which of the two space badgers trapped inside it would survive.

While space badgers can survive and navigate fairly well in vacuums, they really hate water. They can barely swim and their air pack only lasts for a short period of time before they need to refill it in an oxygen rich atmosphere.

There was no way either badger could escape the barrel. A small platform, big enough for just one space badger body, was the only safe haven above waterline. That's what they were fighting for.

The two thrashed about in the water; claws slashing and splashing, glass helmets clinking off each other and the platform. As one badger climbed, the other jumped on top of him, pushing him down under the water.

Each badger had a stripe painted down its back—one was red, the other blue. Red Stripe perched himself firmly atop the platform. Blue Stripe desperately clawed at him from below.

"Gentlemen, we may have ourselves a winner soon," yelled Lieutenant Hanson over the cheering men.

Blue kept trying to climb up to safety but Red swatted him with his strong paws and sent Blue tumbling back into the water. Stunned and tired, he struggled to move. Red's little chest heaved and sighed as he tried to catch his breath.

Blue made one final mad dash at Red, but Red easily caught Blue's helmet between his claws. Blue attempted to thrash free but Red held on tight and smashed Blue's helmet against the platform.

Clink, clink, clink, and then—*CRACK!*

Shards of glass plopped into the water as Blue's helmet shattered. The space badger fell limp. His head began to expand like a balloon until it almost completely filled what was left of the helmet.

POP!

The space badger's head exploded, spraying some of the men standing close by with blood, bone, and brains. They roared even louder.

"Red is the winner, settle up!" yelled Hanson over the cacophony.

Commander Gaines handed two hundred credits over to Hanson.

"Not your lucky day, eh, Commander?" Hanson said, grinning while taking the money.

"I'm lucky when it counts, Lieutenant."

Ensign Walker went to the barrel with a hammer in his hand. The winning space badger was soaking wet and shivering. Its eyes darted around at the crew, pleading, searching in vain for some method of escape. It saw Walker looking at it and swiped its claws along the side of the platform while hissing as loud as it could.

Walker smirked. He raised the hammer above his head and smashed it down on the space badger's helmet. The glass shattered almost completely away—all that remained was a jagged ring of shards around its neck. Its head expanded, and then—*POP*—it exploded.

The normal reward for the winning badger.

"Alright ladies, play time's over," yelled Gaines above the excitement.

The men quieted down and snapped to attention.

"Clean this shit up and get back to work," he continued. "We have a ship to keep working. I'll be on the bridge if anyone needs me."

Gaines grabbed a nearby toolkit and headed to the turbolift. Before reaching the door, he turned back to his men.

"And someone find out where those fucking space badgers are comin' from. Find them and burn them alive."

The U.S.S. Davis was a Super Freighter, capable of transporting several million tons of cargo across more than twice the distance of a standard freighter ship. Commander Gaines had been the chief engineer of the ship for more than two decades. His job was to oversee the ten person engineering department and keep the ship moving, the air flowing, and the gravity going. On most missions, the worst he had to deal with were a few blown out connectors and some loose wires.

The doors to the turbolift opened and Gaines stepped onto the bridge. It wasn't much of a bridge—nothing like the ambassador and war ships had—just a few tech stations that monitored the status of the ship, and a view screen that took up the entire front wall. Right now, it displayed only empty space and pinpoint stars.

Four officers monitored the display screens and Captain Ingles stared at the view screen. Bored.

Gaines went over to the navigation station. Lately it had

been acting up a bit and was calculating their arrival at Depot Station 23 about two hours later than what other calculations were determining. That's not off by much, especially not for the three month mission they were on (transporting 350 million barrels of quadrotriticale). But you really don't want the navigation system acting up at all. The last thing they needed was to get lost, with the nearest starship over fifty systems away.

Gaines kneeled down and popped off the circuit panel. He looked over the mess of wires and bolts but nothing was obviously damaged. That meant he was going to have to check each circuit manually until he found the problem.

Shit. This is going to take hours.

"Captain, a large object has been detected three hundred meters off our starboard bow. About two hundred meters across, four hundred long."

"That's almost as big as us," said the Captain. "How'd it get that close without our sensors picking it up? View screen, now."

A gigantic creature filled the view screen. It looked like a blue whale—the kind of animal one would normally see swimming peacefully on Earth. But this beast had three rows of teeth in its gaping maw. Its body glowed a strange and unnatural neon blue. The monster flapped its four pairs of flippers slowly in space and turned to face the ship.

Gaines had heard of these creatures but he never thought he'd actually see one—a Behemoth.

A spaceman's nightmare, the Behemoth was the most feared creature in space. Nobody really knows how many ships have been lost to Behemoth attacks over the years. The space whales have some way of evading ships' sensors. Only two ships have been known to escape a direct Behemoth attack.

The monster darted forward with astonishing speed straight for the freighter ship.

"Evas—" began the Captain, but was cut off as the ship shook violently. The men on the bridge went tumbling. One of the officers flew head first into the computer screens. His head whipped back and twisted around—snapping his neck. The corpse fell to the floor.

The main lights went out and the emergency lights turned on, bathing everything in a red glow.

Then the female robotic voice of the ship's warning system began. *"Warning. Warning. Extreme structural damage sustained. Engine core overload imminent. Crew is advised to evacuate. Crew is advised to evacuate."* The message repeated itself.

Gaines looked around the bridge and locked eyes with the Captain. There was a large cut across his forehead, spilling blood down his face. The ship shook again as the Behemoth continued its attack.

"You heard the lady," said the Captain, smiling. "Time to—"

His windpipe was crushed before he could finish. The paneling above him gave way and several tons of metal, wire and other duct work fell on top of him, instantly mashing him to a gooey pulp.

Gaines bent down and picked up his toolbox. He wasn't sure why—he just operated on autopilot. He hopped into the turbolift and punched the button for the flight deck. Repeating the steps he had memorized in emergency drills.

When he reached the deck, he had to crawl under metal beams and through loose wires to get into the corridor. He singed his hair on a small fire burning in a fallen air duct. When reached the evacuation area, the escape pod doors all glowed green, indicating that the pods were present and ready to launch. Either Gaines was the first one to get there, or no one else was going to make it off the ship.

He ran straight for the nearest green oval-shaped door and was ten feet away when his feet caught on something and he fell flat on his face. He looked back and saw Lt. Hanson. The officer was trapped beneath a heavy sheet of metal. It covered most of his body, which was why Gaines hadn't seen him lying there. Hanson gripped a hold of Gaines' feet.

"—Warning. Warning. Extreme structural damage sustained—"

The computer continued its alert.

Gaines tried to shake his feet free, but the injured man held tight.

"Let go," yelled Gaines as he kicked.

"Help. . ." Hanson whispered.

There was no time. Gaines swung the toolkit into Hanson's head. There was a loud *crack* and the man moaned. Gaines sat up and brought the metal box down again and again and again. Hanson's body began to convulse and Gaines hit harder and faster. Each blow emitted a wet slushy plop, but still the grip on his feet did not weaken.

"*—Crew is advised to evacuate. Crew is advised to evacuate—*"

He stopped hitting when there was almost no more head left to smash. Gaines reached down and pried the dead man's hands from his feet. Finger by finger.

Gaines stumbled to a standing position, toolkit still in hand, and the ship lurched to one side tossing him into the wall, right next to the pod.

"*Warrrrrrrrrnnnnnnnnn sssssssssssd—*"

The warning system shut off and the red emergency lights went out. The only source of illumination was the green glow of the escape pod doors. Gaines hit the button on the door and it rose up smoothly. He threw himself in and the door slid shut.

The computer system inside the pod whirled to life.

"*Ignition in 3, 2, 1 . . .*"

The pod jerked as it separated from the U.S.S. Davis. Gaines looked out a porthole and saw the Behemoth biting huge chunks out of the freighter. There was almost nothing left of it—nothing worth salvaging anyway.

A blinding flash of white light exploded from the center of the wreckage. Gaines backed away from the porthole rubbing his eyes. They burned, and all he could see were throbbing white clouds.

The pod pitched suddenly. First down and then up, hard. Gaines' feet left the floor and he was hurled through the air. His head hit something and his body crumpled down.

He tried to stand but he could not get his limbs to work. His vision was obscured by white blurs, then grey, then black.

Gaines sat up rubbing the back of his head. His hand brushed a hard bump the size of a walnut and sharp pain shot through his head. He winced and brought his hand where he could see it. Blood. Cradling his head in both hands, he inspected the wound with his fingertips. He gently poked. It felt like an ice pick to the brain every time his fingers made contact but he was relieved to find nothing serious.

He stood up, and while his legs felt wobbly, he didn't appear to be injured in any other way.

He went back to the porthole and looked out. The U.S.S. Davis was gone. Millions of tiny hunks of mangled metal floated aimlessly in space. The engine must have gone nuclear.

There was no sign of the Behemoth.

The interior of the escape pod was about twelve feet wide by twenty feet long with an eight foot clearance. It was one long room with a cockpit with a hyper-strong glass shield surrounding it. The walls were storage cabinets and computer banks; all colored the same shade of metallic gold as the floor and ceiling. The porthole in the docking door was the only other view outside.

Gaines went to the cockpit and sat down. A quick glance at the control panel showed all the pod's systems at normal operational levels. The blast from the ship didn't seem to have damaged the escape pod. Thank God.

He did a scan of the surrounding space for life signs or emergency signals from other escape pods. It took the computer under a minute to complete its operation. Nothing. It appeared that Gaines was the only one who made it off the ship.

He plotted a course for the nearest starbase. It would be a long trip—about two weeks stuck in that tin can. But the pod was stocked with food and water. He would be fine. He finished entering the coordinates and hit ENGAGE.

Nothing happened. ENGINE FAILURE flashed in bright red letters across the screen.

"Shit," he muttered. Maybe the blast *did* damage his pod. According to protocol, his next course of action was to send out a distress call. He recorded a brief message giving his name, title, ship of service, location and request for immediate assistance. When he finished he pushed SEND.

MESSAGE FAILURE.

"Shit!"

He sat back from the panel. He couldn't move the ship and he couldn't call for help. He spun around in the chair to look over the escape pod and see if he could think of anything else to do.

His eyes immediately latched onto the toolkit that was lying on its side in the far corner. He could fix the pod. It might take a while but he knew he could do it.

If he worked quickly, he figured he might still have enough supplies to get him to the starbase, even with the extra time spent fixing the ship. The standard escape pod was stocked with thirty days worth of food and water along with a variety of medical supplies.

Medical supplies . . .

Gaines remembered the lump on the back of his head. He touched it. It still hurt just as bad but the bleeding stopped and the swelling was going down. He should wash it off.

He opened the first cabinet. It was empty. There were a few brown crumbs and an empty energy bar wrapper but nothing else. He went to the next cabinet and opened it—it too was empty. And so were the next two cabinets.

"What the fuck . . ." said Gaines, as he looked from empty cabinet to empty cabinet. Every escape pod was inspected before leaving dock to make sure they were properly outfitted. There's no way this should be possible. Yet here he was.

He had no choice but to get to work on fixing the pod.

He grabbed the toolkit and took out his screwdriver. The access panel to the main circuitry was located in the center of the floor. It was purposefully easy to access just for situations like this. Gaines unscrewed the four bolts that held it in place and hoisted up the heavy metal panel.

At first, he couldn't make sense of what he saw. Where there should have been a mess of wire and motherboards, there was a solid, heaving mass of brown fur. Suddenly a dozen little heads in glass helmets popped up.

Space badgers.

They hissed at Gaines.

He calmly placed the metal panel back in place and screwed the four bolts back in place. He could hear the space badgers on the other side, scratching with their heavy, sharp claws.

He went back to the cockpit and did a scan of his pod for life-signs. A minute went by and then a second minute. After three full minutes had passed and the computer hadn't finished conducting its scan, he began to get worried.

Please don't fail on me too.

After five minutes there was a loud *beep* and the screen read SCAN ERROR—TOO MANY READINGS IN TOO CLOSE PROXIMITY—CANNOT ACQUIRE FIXED SCAN.

Holy fuck, they were nesting in here, Gaines thought.

Scratch, scratch, scratch, scratch.

The noise came from all around him. Gaines heard the space badgers scratch beneath the floor, in the ceiling, and from inside all the walls. When he opened the panel, it must have riled them up.

Gaines sat still, looking around the small cabin that suddenly seemed much smaller, listening to the animals move about. It sounded like there were hundreds of them.

Well, I guess I know what's messing with the pod.

It took him a full hour to thoroughly search the entire pod but he safely, and sadly, confirmed that there was no food or water anywhere on the ship. The space badgers must have ate and drank it all. There were also no medical supplies, tools, or weapons. In fact, there was nothing that wasn't bolted down. Even the emergency space suit was missing. The space badgers had cleaned the pod of everything. Why they did that, Gaines had no clue.

He sat back in his chair and his eyes quickly began to feel very heavy. All the stress and physical exertion were taking their toll on him.

He must have fallen asleep but he snapped awake to the sound of claws scurrying on metal. He looked across the pod and saw four space badgers digging through his toolbox. On the wall next to them, one of the metal panels had been bent forward providing a two foot hole in the wall. Through that, Gaines could see nothing but fur as dozens of space badgers moved within the walls of his pod.

"Hey," he shouted while standing up.

The four space badgers whipped their heads up and turned to face Gaines. Each held a different tool in their claws and they were as still as statues. Suddenly, three of them made a dash for the hole in the wall. The fourth dropped the tool it was holding, grabbed the handle of the toolkit, and ran—trying to take all the tools with it.

Gaines chased after them. By the time he reached the other side of the pod, three of the space badgers had already escaped with their prizes. The fourth was trying to pull the toolkit through the hole but it was too bulky to fit.

Gaines grabbed the kit and pulled back but the space badger would not let go. He accidently hit the latch and the kit spilled open, dumping tools on the floor. Other space badgers darted out of the hole and snatched up the instruments from the floor.

"No no no no," Gaines said. Acting out of reflex, he let go of the kit and tried to scoop up the tools from the floor. Each time he tried to grab one, a space badger claw would shoot out, scratch him, and steal the tool. In moments, the space badgers pulled all the tools through the hole and even the kit itself.

Gaines kicked the bent out metal panel. "Fuck! Fuck! Fuck!" he yelled with each kick as he bent it back into place.

When he'd closed it enough to keep out the space badgers, Gaines slumped to the floor and looked at his hands. They felt like they were on fire. Each one, covered with dozens of bleeding scratches. In some spots, the cuts were so deep that the blood flowed down his fingertips and dripped onto the golden metal floor.

He looked around and saw that the space badgers had missed one tool—the screwdriver. Gaines darted across the floor on his hands and knees and greedily scooped up the tool.

Those Goddamn pests got my food, my water, my medicine, and now my tools. All I got is this fucking screwdriver.

He sat on the floor looking at his one tool. If he was going to get this ship moving again, he needed to figure out how to get all the space badgers out of its interior.

He sat for a full half-hour thinking over the situation, when finally an idea came to him. An absolutely insane idea. But if it worked, he could escape. If it failed, at least he'd be dead sooner that starving or dying of thirst.

He went to work right away. First he addressed the panel the space badgers had bent out. He unscrewed four bolts and it fell to the floor with a *Clang!* Confused space badgers blinked at the bright light from the cabin and half-heartedly hissed at him.

Gaines ran to another wall and unscrewed the first panel he came to. Once it was removed, more confused space badgers spilled out. He unscrewed another panel and another.

Once he removed all six interior wall panels he went to the panel on the floor—the same one where he first discovered the space badger infestation. Now the other badgers had adjusted to the light and were angry at being disturbed. They jumped at his legs and scratched while he unscrewed the final bolts, frantically trying to finish his work.

Finally the last bolt was out. He pulled on the panel and tossed it aside. The interior of the cabin filled with space badgers. They poured out of the openings in the walls and floor.

Gaines kicked the animals aside and made his way across the room to the cockpit. He sat himself down in the chair and strapped all three seat belts—two across his chest and one across his lap.

He pushed buttons on the control panel while space

badgers scratched his legs, tearing open dozens of wounds, and began to climb his command chair.

The screen read OPEN DOCKING DOORS? EMERGENCY OPPERATING OVERRIDE YES/NO.

Gaines took a deep breath and pressed YES.

The docking door began to open. Then all air was violently sucked out of the escape pod. The force spun Gaines' chair around and scores of space badgers flew out the door.

The animals poured from all of the open panels. They just kept coming and coming. Gaines felt his lungs threatening to burst and his eyes felt like they wanted to leap from their sockets.

Finally, the atmosphere seemed empty of space badgers—except for one that had its claws dug into Gaines' calf muscle. The pull of the vacuum wrenched the wounds wider, and the animal still hung on. Gaines kicked at the beast with his other leg. He didn't know how much longer he could hold on. His lungs were screaming but if he tried to take a breath it was all over for him.

Just when Gaines thought he could take no more, the space badger lost its grip and went spiraling through the pod and out the door. Gaines' hands thrashed atop the control panel and hit the button reading CLOSE.

The docking doors lowered shut and immediately, the life support system adjusted the atmosphere to normal. Gaines gasped for breath.

He hit buttons on the control panel starting a full system scan. In moments the screen read SYSTEM SCAN COMPLETE: ALL SYSTEMS NORMAL.

Gaines almost started crying.

It worked. I have control of the ship again.

He replotted the course to the closest starbase. Sure it would take him two weeks, and he didn't know what he was going to do about food, water, or all the open wounds on his body—but at least he was moving.

He paused and looked out the glass screen. All around the ship hundreds of space badgers floated in space. They thrashed about and tried to space-swim their way back to the escape pod or to other hunks of floating debris. It would still be another half an hour before their air ran out and they choked to death. Gaines wished he could stay to watch that.

The stars directly in front of his escape pod suddenly looked very weird. It was like they were shimmering and shaking in place. The area turned a familiar neon blue as a huge mass revealed itself in front of the small ship.

The Behemoth was back. It must have had some kind of camouflage system that enabled it to blend into its space background. Gaines finally solved the mystery of how Behemoths can so easily sneak up on ships.

Not that it mattered.

The monster was attracted to all the space badgers floating around. They had nowhere to escape—and neither did Gaines.

He furiously attempted to finish punching in the coordinates but he was too late. The Behemoth's jaws snapped shut around the escape pod and the hundreds of space badgers.

Marx, Split-Tail, Gonzo, and Johnny McRazor were the most badass punk rockers in the Merciful Hearts Nursing Home. They were all over eighty, but they still wore black leather jackets hand-painted with punk band logos and anarchist slogans. And they never went anywhere without their black jeans and black combat boots.

Marx covered his dialysis machine with stickers proclaiming "Kill Whitey," "Burn the Rich," and his personal favorite, "Kill Cops."

Split-Tail dyed his waist-length hair to match his spray-painted walker.

Gonzo had metal screw-in spikes encircling his bald head like a crown.

Johnny had diabetes. He liked to inject his insulin in a public place and pretend to enter the bliss of a heroin stupor, or go into seizures from an overdose. None of the other nursing home residents found this amusing.

They were once the greatest punk band of their day.

Marx, Split-Tail, Gonzo, and Johnny McRazor all met in high school. They bonded over a love for punk rock and drugs. By the time they graduated, they had already self-released three EPs. On their first US tour playing a variety of squats, firehalls, and dive bars, they caught the attention of Satan Dance Squad Records while playing the Mr. Roboto Project in Pittsburgh. Their first full-length came out later that year.

Soon they were making enough money touring and releasing music that they quit their day jobs at the Piggly Wiggly.

They toured with all the greats back in the day. Mouthful of Ants, Night Gaunts, Chainsaw Millipede, The Stupid Stupid Henchmen—you name the band and they rocked out and got drunk with them.

Then those life-altering things that normally happen to people happened to them.

Love. Kids. A mortgage.

But they didn't sell out. They didn't have to. With the royalties from the twenty-eight studio albums, four live albums, and more compilation appearances than they could count, they were financially secure for the rest of their days. But divorces happen, people die, and kids move out.

And that's where we find them now. Just like the good old days, it's just the four of them, though Merciful Hearts Nursing Home is a little different than Fifth Street.

The four of them were hanging out around the organic garden. Gonzo smoked a cigarette while Johnny, Marx, and Split-Tail passed around a joint.

Nurse Myers appeared next to them.

"Now Mr. Jameson, we can't have you doing that. It's illegal," she said as she snatched the joint from Marx.

"Fuck the Po-Po."

Nurse Myers walked off with their drugs. She was always harshing their buzz.

"Man, I'm sick of this shit," said Johnny. "Can't even get high."

"Eh, what you gonna do?" said Split-Tail.

"There's nothing to ever do around this place," complained Marx.

"Not this again," Johnny sighed. "We go through this every day. I'm fucking tired of this conversation. Come on, I got some hash brownies in my room. Let's go watch some Doctor Who."

"Nah," said Split-Tail, "I'm sick of watching TV."

"So what do you want to do?" asked Johnny.

Split-Tail shrugged.

The four of them stood silent for a moment. Gonzo took a drag on his cigarette. "Let's play a show," he said.

"Not this again," said Johnny.

"Come on, why not?"

"Man, you can't even stand up on your own. Marx over there is attached to a fucking dialysis machine."

"You all said it yourselves, there's nothing to fucking do around here."

"Maybe we should," said Marx.

"Fuckin' A, man!" said Gonzo.

"We're too old," said Johnny.

"Shit man," said Split-Tail, shaking his head, "I can't believe I just heard you say that. Just to fucking spite you, I'm in."

"That's three to one," said Gonzo.

Johnny pulled out a cigarette and mumbled "motherfuckers" under his breath. "OK, fuck it, one last time."

Getting back into the habit of the band was like getting back onto a bike (assuming that you could ride a bike, which Split-Tail could not). It was amazing how quickly all their old songs came back to them. "Killing Cops with Lead Pipes," "Zombies Ate All My Cap'n Crunch," and all the others.

After two months of practice, the band was ready. Sure, they played a little slower than they did in the old days but they felt better than they had in decades. It brought back a spark that had been missing through all the years of family life and retirement.

They rented the nursing home auditorium for their reunion show. The only step left was to get the word out.

They printed up cheap photocopied flyers of a collage depicting George W. Bush pissing on the monk protester from Vietnam who set himself on fire, surrounded by a bunch of pentagrams and upside-down crosses.

"Damn good work," said Johnny, looking over the flyer.

"Thanks," said Gonzo, "it's been awhile since I've done one of these." He always made the flyers back in the day.

"I'll hang up a bunch around the place," said Split-Tail, picking up a stack of flyers.

"We're gonna have to hit up some shows over the next couple of weeks to get the word out," said Marx.

"What do you think punk shows are like now?" asked Gonzo.

That Friday, they went to a local punk night at a dive bar called Branx.

"I don't get it," said Gonzo at the back of the venue.

There were no gauged ears, there were no patched-up

119

jackets, and there wasn't even one Mohawk in the entire venue. Not even a spike to be seen.

The band onstage was less punk than a spandex leggings sale at American Apparel. Their name was Strolling Through the Flowers. They played songs about market analysis on three guitars and a theremin.

"I know we've been out of the scene for awhile but..." Marx trailed off.

Split-Tail nodded and then turned to the rest of them, "I'm gonna go give some flyers to the bartender."

He pushed his walker over to the bar.

"What can I get you old man?" asked the bartender.

"I got some flyers for a show coming up. Can you hang them around?"

The bartender took the flyers. He registered a knowing look. "Yeah, I remember those guys. I think my dad used to listen to them."

"Yeah, I'm in them," said Split-Tail, "we got a reunion."

"OK, cool. I'll hang them up."

Split-Tail shuffled back to the others, who were staring in disbelief at the band onstage.

"You know what this means?" asked Johnny.

"Huh?"

"We gotta put on a fucking show for these people."

Over the next four weeks they canvassed the town with flyers and practiced harder than ever before. After seeing the sad affair that was the Strolling Through the Flowers show, and every other show they went to while flyering, they knew they had to give the people a dose of that old classic punk rock.

Finally the night of the show came and the auditorium was packed. All the punks in town, and all of the nursing home residents, had come out to see them play.

The crowd was an even split between twenty-something's and seventy-something's. Everyone was uncomfortable and a little confused. The young people were pissed about the lack of alcohol (the nursing home didn't have a bar), and all the chairs had been removed from the activity center, so there was no place for the nursing home residents to sit down.

The band shuffled onstage. Split-Tail pushed his walker over to the drum kit. Marx set up his dialysis machine next to his bass amp, two tubes trailing from him arm keeping him hooked to the machine. One tube was filled with blood and the other with a yellowish liquid that glowed under the light. Gonzo adjusted the screw-in spikes on his head and slung his old guitar across his chest.

The lights dimmed and Johnny took the stage. His brittle bones caused him to hobble a little, but he still had swagger. He grabbed the mike at the center of the stage and screamed "Fuck you!" at the audience and the band kicked into their first song, "Killing Kittens for Fun and Profit."

The first song was a disaster. The four old punks had done great in rehearsal but they were rusty playing in front of a live audience. When Marx switched on his amp, it interfered with the hearing aids of the nursing home residents causing a painful high pitched feedback noise for several ear-piercing minutes. The audience covered their ears in unison. Nurses raced around the room trying to help the senior citizens. The band powered through the song but a couple of people in the back left before they even reached the chorus.

During the second song, the crowd started to warm up a little. A couple of old men with mohawks drove their electric wheelchairs into the center of the room and started slamming each other like bumper cars. The young people thought it was hilarious and circled around cheering them on.

Johnny flashed devil horns at the audience and winked at a blue-haired old lady bobbing her head in the front row.

Gonzo looked down from the stage and noticed an acne-faced boy covertly pulling a bottle of beer out of his voluminous black raver pants. He reached down and grabbed the beer from the kid. Gonzo raised it up to his forehead, and in his signature style, deftly opened the bottle against one of his spiked implants. While still playing the bass, he chugged the beer and then smashed the bottle on Marx's dialysis machine.

This caused something magical to happen in the minds of the residents of the nursing home. Memories of old nu-metal shows, hardcore matinees, Warped Tour, and Ozzfest flashed through their minds.

They drifted to the front of the auditorium. At first they just nodded their heads to the beat but when the next song began, someone in the center started pushing. Soon the whole crowd was bumping into each other and then a full-on mosh pit had started. At least, as enthusiastic a mosh pit as a seventy-plus-year-old crowd could muster.

Marx wailed on his bass. He lay down on the floor and started to spin in a circle on his back using his legs to push him around the stage. The tubes connecting him to his dialysis machine became tangled and when he stood up, he yanked the yellow tube out of his wrist, spraying the audience with contaminated dialysis fluid.

The crowd screamed and the band started rocking even harder. As they belted out each song the crowd bobbed, feebly slam danced, and flashed devil horns. The young locals stood in the back staring in shock, horror, and confusion.

At the end of the final song of the final encore, "Do Drugs, Kill Cops, Burn Churches"—an old crowd favorite, Johnny was overridden with a sense of freedom. He had forgotten the rush of being onstage. The high from holding the adoration of hundreds of people. The thrill of becoming someone different, someone cooler, than his normal self—at least for an hour and a half. As the band played, he shuffled to the end of the stage and jumped off.

The crowd held up their arms to catch him but age and osteoporosis had made their bones brittle. When Johnny landed, the sounds of bones snapping could be heard even over the music.

His body plummeted straight to the ground and he felt his bones break in two dozen places. The crowd parted around him and Johnny groaned in pain. The band, noticing that something had happened and their front man was now missing, stopped playing. All eyes were on Johnny.

He struggled, and weakly raised one hand and his middle finger.

The band never played together again.

***

Johnny McRazor, now bed-ridden, renamed himself Johnny WhiteNoize and started a one-man experimental act called Screaming Geezer. It was him using a laptop as a sampler while banging on a bedpan for percussion. Gonzo formed a new band with some of the guys in the shuffle board league. They said they played crust-punk but everyone agreed it sounded like metal. Split-Tail dreaded his hair and started doing reggae dub remixes under the name King See-Zar. He spun classic ska, roots, dub, and dancehall every Wednesday night in the Merciful Hearts Nursing Home activity center, and every Friday at the Red Room. Marx, much to everyone's shame, got really into Dubstep.

Exactly one year to the day from their final show, all four of them died. Their bodies were found by orderlies in their beds. All four passed on peacefully in their sleep. Some say that they achieved punk rock godhood that fateful night, and heaven wanted its turn at some sweet circle pits. Others say they sold their souls to Satan to rock so hard and that night the devil came for what was his. Still others blame the carbon monoxide leak that was later discovered and also killed six other residents that night.

The truth doesn't matter.

What does matter is their funeral. As per their wills, a combined funeral for all four of them was held. It was one big party. Held at a firehall (instead of a funeral home), it was open to all and, throughout the day, hundreds of people showed up. People brought booze and weed and soon everyone was drunk and stoned—just as their last wishes dictated.

Some bands showed up and played sets in honor of their fallen comrades. The reformed Mouthful of Ants even played a surprise set (though, in all fairness, only one original member was still alive). "This one goes out to the four guys in boxes," yelled Kiichi at the start of their first song.

At the end of the night everyone passed by the coffins and placed offerings of beer, weed, and cigarettes in with the bodies. And then, one by one, people went up to the microphone and said their eulogies. Everyone had different stories of how the band had affected their lives. For some, they had been saved from a life of drugs, bad sex, and depression. For others, the music had led them to a life of drugs, great sex, and good times. Everyone agreed that the band had inspired them to improve their lives.

And everyone agreed that the band's final show at the Merciful Hearts Nursing Home activity center was the best set they'd ever played.

"But how do you account for the natural disconnect inherent between all people?"

"Eeeee aaaa gggghhhh iiiiiaaa," replied the derelict while rolling back his eyes. Drool dribbled down his dreaded beard and slowly drip, drip, dripped onto his handmade cardboard sign.

Ronald looked one last time at the childlike scrawl, *Free Nachos, Free Beers, Free Tibet.* With a "humph", he turned and walked deeper into the park.

On every available six cubic feet of grass stood a philosopher espousing the hidden truths of the world. Ronald strolled along and breathed in the clean spring air, looking for a worthwhile opponent to debate.

To his right, a couple lounged while their two small children ran about throwing rotten strawberries at a man who was wildly waving his arms and jabbering about the space-time continuum. To his left stood a well-dressed man in a black suit, arms stretching to the sky waving dollar-bills at beings only he could see. Ronald had debated him two weeks ago—it had just degenerated into a three hour screaming fit.

Everyday for sixteen years he had come to the park, and it was becoming tedious. Before, he could come and dispute the intricacies of the universe for hours on end, but now he could not even find a decent conversation about the weather. Ronald had already argued with everyone in the park, most several times over.

As he walked further into the park he overheard retorts and accusations he himself had once said. When he approached the thick patch of trees in the back, he stared at them and quickly got lost in self-pity.

Through a hole in the overgrown vegetation he noticed a flapping piece of white cloth. The trees were so tightly packed, that, as he approached, he could not make out exactly what he was seeing. Curious over what this could be, and already having given up hope of discussion for the day, Ronald pushed his way through.

He stepped into a clearing circled by the thick mass of

brush. In the center a woman stood atop a two-foot wooden crate holding a crisp, blank piece of cardboard. Her hair and face were smeared with dirt and all she wore was a long once-upon-a-time-white dress. Except for the small hole through which Ronald had glimpsed a flapping part of the dress, all the sights and sounds of the park were blocked out by the plant life.

In the numerous times he had been in the park, Ronald had never found this clearing and he had never debated this woman.

"How interesting," he eagerly said, approaching the woman and pointing to her blank sign, "What statement are you attempting to make?"

The woman stared straight ahead and did not respond.

Ronald spoke again, louder, "What is your point?"

Still no response.

"Come now, why are you here? You must have something to say." He regarded the strange woman for a few moments and then began to rattle off guesses, hoping one would be the instigator for a vigorous debate.

"A statement on the pointlessness of life?"

"A protest against the commercialization of art?"

"An acknowledgment of one's place in the universe?"

No matter what theory Ronald put forth, the woman gave no acknowledgement.

"I know—you're alluding to Plato's theory of the forms and how all reality is inherently unreal."

Nothing. The woman just continued to stare off.

Ronald rubbed his chin, taking special notice of his carefully trimmed whiskers. He walked behind and then around the woman, but suffered no stroke of genius.

"I'm going to figure you out," he said stabbing his finger at her. "I'm going to sit down right here and not leave until I do."

And that is what he did. He sat down on the grass and stared at her, thinking. He sat there that day and night. He sat there through the next day and night. On the third day, through sleep deprivation and hunger delirium, the answer came to Ronald. He leapt to his feet to proclaim the sudden truth.

"Rrrrrr gggghhhttt." He frantically looked about in confusion as random noise came spewing from his mouth, "Kkkkk bbvvvveeee."

Stepping down from the box, the woman looked into Ronald's eyes with equal parts compassion and pity. She placed her hands on his shoulders and carefully guided him to stand atop the box. She handed him the piece of cardboard and a marker she gracefully produced from beneath her dress, both of which he eagerly snatched up. With a fury he began to scrawl on the cardboard. The woman turned away before he was finished writing. There was no need to read it.

As she pushed her way through the trees, Ronald stood atop his pedestal blabbering to no one. The grass tickled her feet as she walked to the exit of the park. To her left a couple was asleep on the grass while their two children were elbow deep in the chest cavity of a corpse. Joyously grabbing handfuls of viscera and tossing it into the air, laughing in their gore shower. To her right a well-dressed man in a black suit tossed crumpled dollar-bills into the air. One after another they vanished as if gobbled up by invisible mouths.

"Good day, Ma'am," said the park guard while tipping his hat to the woman. She smiled and nodded and walked out of the park. She would be back tomorrow, but now she needed another box and more cardboard.

ABOUT THE STORIES

Cripple Wolf

One day I was hanging out and drinking with Cameron Pierce and Carlton Mellick III. I had just watched an episode of "Fringe." The show opened with a person transforming into a werewolf-like creature on an airplane. The scene was super badass. But then the opening credits rolled and the episode resumed with the main characters of the series finding out the airplane had crashed and the rest of the episode dealt with the investigation into the disaster.

The show sucked but I was fascinated with the idea of a werewolf on an airplane. I thought it sounded like an awesome premise for a story. But how does the werewolf not kill everyone in five minutes?

I presented this question to Cameron and Carlton. Cameron said, "Put the werewolf in a wheelchair."

The three of us thought the idea was hilarious. The basic plot of "Cripple Wolf" was generated right there. I ran with it and, a few months later, I wrote this story.

Frosty and the Full Monty

I really hate Christmas. Or, to be more specific, I really hate the Christmas season. I can't stand the gaudy lights, the cheap plastic decorations, the mind-numbingly repetitive music, and the glorification of material goods. I just can't stand the entire Christmas aesthetic.

When Carlton Mellick III was putting together his *Christmas on Crack* anthology, I jumped at a chance to write a story for it. I'm not sure why I picked Frosty for the topic. I think it's mostly because I didn't want to have to write a story about Jesus or Santa—I just couldn't bear to do that.

My Mom loves the Christmas season. Quite frankly, she's rather obsessed. Every holiday season growing up it was a winter wonderland in my house with decorations and non-stop Christmas music.

I kind of feel bad for what I did to Frosty in this story because of my mom. She doesn't know this story exists. *Shhhhhh…*nobody tell her.

Cook for Your Life

I don't like reality shows and I don't like game shows, however, I think competitive cooking shows are awesome. Iron Chef is my favorite of those types of shows. This story is my tribute to it and especially that crazy Japanese guy with the sword that opens almost every episode. He's crazy.

House of Cats

I live in Portland, Oregon. I love the city so much. I've been fortunate enough to have spent time in cities all over the United States and the world. But no place makes me feel more welcome and at home than Portland.

One of the many quirky aspects of this city is how it is overrun with cats. In most cities you find junkies and dealers hanging on the street corners. In Portland, you see cats.

I have two ideas of what to do with all these excess cats. The first idea is to make cardboard suits of armor for the cats. I would then spend a few days catching as many cats around the city that I could and outfit them all in the armor. The goal would be to create the impression there was a city-wide cat turf war. It would be like the cats were going all Mad Max on each other and shit.

The second idea was this story.

Adrift with Space Badgers

There are three big artistic influences from my youth that made me into the person I am today—Star Trek, Godzilla movies, and E.C. Comics. Everyone knows what the first two are but a lot of people seem to be unfamiliar with E.C. They were a comic book company from the nineteen-fifties that specialized in very bloody and gory horror, science-fiction, and crime stories. They had titles like *The Haunt of Fear*, *Weird Science-Fantasy*, *Shock SuspenStories*, and, their most famous title, *Tales from the Crypt*. That's right—the awesome TV show is actually based on a series of gory comic books from the fifties.

I had already done my tributes to Star Trek and Godzilla (*Shatnerquake* and *Super Giant Monster Time!* respectively). "Adrift with Space Badgers" is my tribute to E.C.

Basically this story is a bizarro rewrite of two *Tales from the Crypt* stories—"Survival or Death" by Al Feldsein and Jack Davis from *Tales from the Crypt* #31 and "Telescope" by Jack Davis from *Tales from the Crypt* #45.

Punk Rock Nursing Home

A constant question/joke in the punk scene is what's going to happen to punk rockers when they get old? Will they hang up their patched-up jackets and finally shave off the Mohawks or will they still be rocking out while old, gray, and wrinkly? No one really knows yet—punks have a bad habit of dying before they get old.

This story is my humorous take on a punk rock band that somehow manages to never sell out or get old at heart.

Just Another Day in the Park

This is the oldest story in the collection and the first thing I ever wrote that other people liked. Before this I had been trying to be a horror writer. While I love the genre, I couldn't write a decent horror story to save my life. After several years of being a shitty unpublished horror writer, I decided to try writing stuff that was just plain "weird" (I hadn't yet discovered the bizarro scene).

It took me three years to get this piece published—which was in Cameron Pierce's short lived but awesome zine *Furniture Fangs*.

Jeff Burk (left) with Wrath James White (right)

JEFF BURK lives in Portland, OR. He is the author of the cult hit *Shatnerquake* and the choose-your-own-mind-fuck-fest *Super Giant Monster Time!* He is the Head Editor of Deadite Press and the Editor-in-Chief of the Magazine of Bizarro Fiction. He once went undefeated in a professional level Magic: The Gathering tournament.

Bizarro books

CATALOG SPRING 2011

Bizarro Books publishes under the following imprints:

www.rawdogscreamingpress.com

www.eraserheadpress.com

www.afterbirthbooks.com

www.swallowdownpress.com

For all your Bizarro needs visit:

WWW.BIZARROCENTRAL.COM

Introduce yourselves to the bizarro fiction genre and all of its authors with the Bizarro Starter Kit series. Each volume features short novels and short stories by ten of the leading bizarro authors, designed to give you a perfect sampling of the genre for only $10.

BB-0X1
"The Bizarro Starter Kit"
(Orange)
Featuring D. Harlan Wilson, Carlton Mellick III, Jeremy Robert Johnson, Kevin L Donihe, Gina Ranalli, Andre Duza, Vincent W. Sakowski, Steve Beard, John Edward Lawson, and Bruce Taylor.
236 pages $10

BB-0X2
"The Bizarro Starter Kit"
(Blue)
Featuring Ray Fracalossy, Jeremy C. Shipp, Jordan Krall, Mykle Hansen, Andersen Prunty, Eckhard Gerdes, Bradley Sands, Steve Aylett, Christian TeBordo, and Tony Rauch. **244 pages $10**

BB-0X2
"The Bizarro Starter Kit"
(Purple)
Featuring Russell Edson, Athena Villaverde, David Agranoff, Matthew Revert, Andrew Goldfarb, Jeff Burk, Garrett Cook, Kris Saknussemm, Cody Goodfellow, and Cameron Pierce **264 pages $10**

BB-001 **"The Kafka Effekt" D. Harlan Wilson** - A collection of forty-four irreal short stories loosely written in the vein of Franz Kafka, with more than a pinch of William S. Burroughs sprinkled on top. **211 pages $14**

BB-002 **"Satan Burger" Carlton Mellick III** - The cult novel that put Carlton Mellick III on the map ... Six punks get jobs at a fast food restaurant owned by the devil in a city violently overpopulated by surreal alien cultures. **236 pages $14**

BB-003 **"Some Things Are Better Left Unplugged" Vincent Sakwoski** - Join The Man and his Nemesis, the obese tabby, for a nightmare roller coaster ride into this postmodern fantasy. **152 pages $10**

BB-004 **"Shall We Gather At the Garden?" Kevin L Donihe** - Donihe's Debut novel. Midgets take over the world, The Church of Lionel Richie vs. The Church of the Byrds, plant porn and more! **244 pages $14**

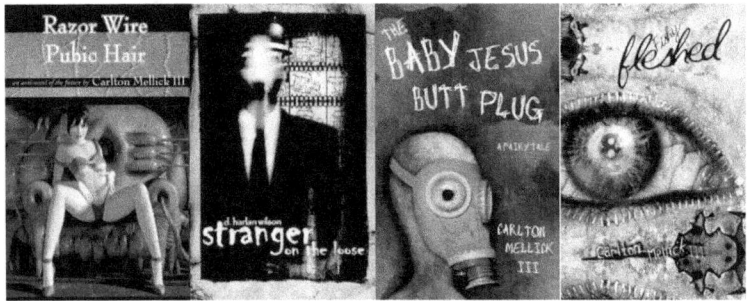

BB-005 **"Razor Wire Pubic Hair" Carlton Mellick III** - A genderless humandildo is purchased by a razor dominatrix and brought into her nightmarish world of bizarre sex and mutilation. **176 pages $11**

BB-006 **"Stranger on the Loose" D. Harlan Wilson** - The fiction of Wilson's 2nd collection is planted in the soil of normalcy, but what grows out of that soil is a dark, witty, otherworldly jungle... **228 pages $14**

BB-007 **"The Baby Jesus Butt Plug" Carlton Mellick III** - Using clones of the Baby Jesus for anal sex will be the hip sex fetish of the future. **92 pages $10**

BB-008 **"Fishyfleshed" Carlton Mellick III** - The world of the past is an illogical flatland lacking in dimension and color, a sick-scape of crispy squid people wandering the desert for no apparent reason. **260 pages $14**

BB-009 **"Dead Bitch Army" Andre Duza** - Step into a world filled with racist teenagers, cannibals, 100 warped Uncle Sams, automobiles with razor-sharp teeth, living graffiti, and a pissed-off zombie bitch out for revenge. **344 pages $16**

BB-010 **"The Menstruating Mall" Carlton Mellick III** - "The Breakfast Club meets Chopping Mall as directed by David Lynch." - Brian Keene **212 pages $12**

BB-011 **"Angel Dust Apocalypse" Jeremy Robert Johnson** - Meth-heads, man-made monsters, and murderous Neo-Nazis. "Seriously amazing short stories..." - Chuck Palahniuk, author of Fight Club **184 pages $11**

BB-012 **"Ocean of Lard" Kevin L Donihe / Carlton Mellick III** - A parody of those old Choose Your Own Adventure kid's books about some very odd pirates sailing on a sea made of animal fat. **176 pages $12**

BB-015 **"Foop!" Chris Genoa** - Strange happenings are going on at Dactyl, Inc, the world's first and only time travel tourism company. "A surreal pie in the face!" - Christopher Moore **300 pages $14**

BB-020 **"Punk Land" Carlton Mellick III** - In the punk version of Heaven, the anarchist utopia is threatened by corporate fascism and only Goblin, Mortician's sperm, and a blue-mohawked female assassin named Shark Girl can stop them. **284 pages $15**

BB-021**"Pseudo-City" D. Harlan Wilson** - Pseudo-City exposes what waits in the bathroom stall, under the manhole cover and in the corporate boardroom, all in a way that can only be described as mind-bogglingly irreal. **220 pages $16**

BB-023 **"Sex and Death In Television Town" Carlton Mellick III** - In the old west, a gang of hermaphrodite gunslingers take refuge from a demon plague in Telos: a town where its citizens have televisions instead of heads. **184 pages $12**

BB-027 **"Siren Promised" Jeremy Robert Johnson & Alan M Clark**
- Nominated for the Bram Stoker Award. A potent mix of bad drugs, bad dreams, brutal bad guys, and surreal/incredible art by Alan M. Clark. **190 pages $13**

BB-030 **"Grape City" Kevin L. Donihe** - More Donihe-style comedic bizarro about a demon named Charles who is forced to work a minimum wage job on Earth after Hell goes out of business. **108 pages $10**

BB-031**"Sea of the Patchwork Cats" Carlton Mellick III** - A quiet dreamlike tale set in the ashes of the human race. For Mellick enthusiasts who also adore The Twilight Zone. **112 pages $10**

BB-032 **"Extinction Journals" Jeremy Robert Johnson** - An uncanny voyage across a newly nuclear America where one man must confront the problems associated with loneliness, insane dieties, radiation, love, and an ever-evolving cockroach suit with a mind of its own. **104 pages $10**

BB-034 **"The Greatest Fucking Moment in Sports" Kevin L. Donihe**
- In the tradition of the surreal anti-sitcom Get A Life comes a tale of triumph and agape love from the master of comedic bizarro. **108 pages $10**

BB-035 **"The Troublesome Amputee" John Edward Lawson** - Disturbing verse from a man who truly believes nothing is sacred and intends to prove it. **104 pages $9**

BB-037 **"The Haunted Vagina" Carlton Mellick III** - It's difficult to love a woman whose vagina is a gateway to the world of the dead. **132 pages $10**

BB-042 **"Teeth and Tongue Landscape" Carlton Mellick III** - On a planet made out of meat, a socially-obsessive monophobic man tries to find his place amongst the strange creatures and communities that he comes across. **110 pages $10**

BB-043 **"War Slut" Carlton Mellick III** - Part "1984," part "Waiting for Godot," and part action horror video game adaptation of John Carpenter's "The Thing." **116 pages $10**

BB-045 **"Dr. Identity" D. Harlan Wilson** - Follow the Dystopian Duo on a killing spree of epic proportions through the irreal postcapitalist city of Bliptown where time ticks sideways, artificial Bug-Eyed Monsters punish citizens for consumer-capitalist lethargy, and ultraviolence is as essential as a daily multivitamin. **208 pages $15**

BB-047 **"Sausagey Santa" Carlton Mellick III** - A bizarro Christmas tale featuring Santa as a piratey mutant with a body made of sausages. 124 pages $10

BB-048 **"Misadventures in a Thumbnail Universe" Vincent Sakowski** - Dive deep into the surreal and satirical realms of neo-classical Blender Fiction, filled with television shoes and flesh-filled skies. **120 pages $10**

BB-049 **"Vacation" Jeremy C. Shipp** - Blueblood Bernard Johnson leaved his boring life behind to go on The Vacation, a year-long corporate sponsored odyssey. But instead of seeing the world, Bernard is captured by terrorists, becomes a key figure in secret drug wars, and, worse, doesn't once miss his secure American Dream. **160 pages $14**

BB-053 **"Ballad of a Slow Poisoner" Andrew Goldfarb** Millford Mutterwurst sat down on a Tuesday to take his afternoon tea, and made the unpleasant discovery that his elbows were becoming flatter. **128 pages $10**

BB-055 **"Help! A Bear is Eating Me" Mykle Hansen** - The bizarro, heartwarming, magical tale of poor planning, hubris and severe blood loss...
150 pages $11

BB-056 **"Piecemeal June" Jordan Krall** - A man falls in love with a living sex doll, but with love comes danger when her creator comes after her with crab-squid assassins. **90 pages $9**

BB-058 **"The Overwhelming Urge" Andersen Prunty** - A collection of bizarro tales by Andersen Prunty. **150 pages $11**

BB-059 **"Adolf in Wonderland" Carlton Mellick III** - A dreamlike adventure that takes a young descendant of Adolf Hitler's design and sends him down the rabbit hole into a world of imperfection and disorder. **180 pages $11**

BB-061 **"Ultra Fuckers" Carlton Mellick III** - Absurdist suburban horror about a couple who enter an upper middle class gated community but can't find their way out. **108 pages $9**

BB-062 **"House of Houses" Kevin L. Donihe** - An odd man wants to marry his house. Unfortunately, all of the houses in the world collapse at the same time in the Great House Holocaust. Now he must travel to House Heaven to find his departed fiancee. **172 pages $11**

BB-064 **"Squid Pulp Blues" Jordan Krall** - In these three bizarro-noir novellas, the reader is thrown into a world of murderers, drugs made from squid parts, deformed gun-toting veterans, and a mischievous apocalyptic donkey. **204 pages $12**

BB-065 **"Jack and Mr. Grin" Andersen Prunty** - "When Mr. Grin calls you can hear a smile in his voice. Not a warm and friendly smile, but the kind that seizes your spine in fear. You don't need to pay your phone bill to hear it. That smile is in every line of Prunty's prose." - Tom Bradley. **208 pages $12**

BB-066 **"Cybernetrix" Carlton Mellick III** - What would you do if your normal everyday world was slowly mutating into the video game world from Tron? **212 pages $12**

BB-072 **"Zerostrata" Andersen Prunty** - Hansel Nothing lives in a tree house, suffers from memory loss, has a very eccentric family, and falls in love with a woman who runs naked through the woods every night. **144 pages $11**

BB-073 "The Egg Man" Carlton Mellick III - It is a world where humans reproduce like insects. Children are the property of corporations, and having an enormous ten-foot brain implanted into your skull is a grotesque sexual fetish. Mellick's industrial urban dystopia is one of his darkest and grittiest to date. **184 pages $11**

BB-074 "Shark Hunting in Paradise Garden" Cameron Pierce - A group of strange humanoid religious fanatics travel back in time to the Garden of Eden to discover it is invested with hundreds of giant flying maneating sharks. **150 pages $10**

BB-075 "Apeshit" Carlton Mellick III - Friday the 13th meets Visitor Q. Six hipster teens go to a cabin in the woods inhabited by a deformed killer. An incredibly fucked-up parody of B-horror movies with a bizarro slant. **192 pages $12**

BB-076 "Fuckers of Everything on the Crazy Shitting Planet of the Vomit At mosphere" Mykle Hansen - Three bizarro satires. Monster Cocks, Journey to the Center of Agnes Cuddlebottom, and Crazy Shitting Planet. **228 pages $12**

BB-077 "The Kissing Bug" Daniel Scott Buck - In the tradition of Roald Dahl, Tim Burton, and Edward Gorey, comes this bizarro anti-war children's story about a bohemian conenose kissing bug who falls in love with a human woman. **116 pages $10**

BB-078 "MachoPoni" Lotus Rose - It's My Little Pony... *Bizarro* style! A long time ago Poniworld was split in two. On one side of the Jagged Line is the Pastel King-dom, a magical land of music, parties, and positivity. On the other side of the Jagged Line is Dark Kingdom inhabited by an army of undead ponies. **148 pages $11**

BB-079 "The Faggiest Vampire" Carlton Mellick III - A Roald Dahl-esque children's story about two faggy vampires who partake in a mustache competition to find out which one is truly the faggiest. **104 pages $10**

BB-080 "Sky Tongues" Gina Ranalli - The autobiography of Sky Tongues, the biracial hermaphrodite actress with tongues for fingers. Follow her strange life story as she rises from freak to fame. **204 pages $12**

BB-081 **"Washer Mouth" Kevin L. Donihe** - A washing machine becomes human and pursues his dream of meeting his favorite soap opera star. **244 pages $11**

BB-082 **"Shatnerquake" Jeff Burk** - All of the characters ever played by William Shatner are suddenly sucked into our world. Their mission: hunt down and destroy the real William Shatner. **100 pages $10**

BB-083 **"The Cannibals of Candyland" Carlton Mellick III** - There exists a race of cannibals that are made of candy. They live in an underground world made out of candy. One man has dedicated his life to killing them all. **170 pages $11**

BB-084 **"Slub Glub in the Weird World of the Weeping Willows"**
Andrew Goldfarb - The charming tale of a blue glob named Slub Glub who helps the weeping willows whose tears are flooding the earth. There are also hyenas, ghosts, and a voodoo priest **100 pages $10**

BB-085 **"Super Fetus" Adam Pepper** - Try to abort this fetus and he'll kick your ass! **104 pages $10**

BB-086 **"Fistful of Feet" Jordan Krall** - A bizarro tribute to spaghetti westerns, featuring Cthulhu-worshipping Indians, a woman with four feet, a crazed gunman who is obsessed with sucking on candy, Syphilis-ridden mutants, sexually transmitted tattoos, and a house devoted to the freakiest fetishes. **228 pages $12**

BB-087 **"Ass Goblins of Auschwitz" Cameron Pierce** - It's Monty Python meets Nazi exploitation in a surreal nightmare as can only be imagined by Bizarro author Cameron Pierce. **104 pages $10**

BB-088 **"Silent Weapons for Quiet Wars" Cody Goodfellow** - "This is high-end psychological surrealist horror meets bottom-feeding low-life crime in a techno-thrilling science fiction world full of Lovecraft and magic..." -John Skipp
212 pages $12

BB-089 "Warrior Wolf Women of the Wasteland" Carlton Mellick III
Road Warrior Werewolves versus McDonaldland Mutants...post-apocalyptic fiction has never been quite like this. **316 pages $13**

BB-090 "Cursed" Jeremy C Shipp - The story of a group of characters who believe they are cursed and attempt to figure out who cursed them and why. A tale of stylish absurdism and suspenseful horror. **218 pages $15**

BB-091 "Super Giant Monster Time" Jeff Burk - A tribute to choose your own adventures and Godzilla movies. Will you escape the giant monsters that are rampaging the fuck out of your city and shit? Or will you join the mob of alien-controlled punk rockers causing chaos in the streets? What happens next depends on you. **188 pages $12**

BB-092 "Perfect Union" Cody Goodfellow - "Cronenberg's THE FLY on a grand scale: human/insect gene-spliced body horror, where the human hive politics are as shocking as the gore." -John Skipp. **272 pages $13**

BB-093 "Sunset with a Beard" Carlton Mellick III - 14 stories of surreal science fiction. **200 pages $12**

BB-094 "My Fake War" Andersen Prunty - The absurd tale of an unlikely soldier forced to fight a war that, quite possibly, does not exist. It's Rambo meets Waiting for Godot in this subversive satire of American values and the scope of the human imagination. **128 pages $11**

BB-095 "Lost in Cat Brain Land" Cameron Pierce - Sad stories from a surreal world. A fascist mustache, the ghost of Franz Kafka, a desert inside a dead cat. Primordial entities mourn the death of their child. The desperate serve tea to mysterious creatures. A hopeless romantic falls in love with a pterodactyl. And much more. **152 pages $11**

BB-096 "The Kobold Wizard's Dildo of Enlightenment +2" Carlton Mellick III - A Dungeons and Dragons parody about a group of people who learn they are only made up characters in an AD&D campaign and must find a way to resist their nerdy teenaged players and retarded dungeon master in order to survive. 232 **pages $12**

BB-097 **"My Heart Said No, but the Camera Crew Said Yes!" Bradley Sands** - A collection of short stories that are crammed with the delightfully odd and the scurrilously silly. **140 pages $13**

BB-098 **"A Hundred Horrible Sorrows of Ogner Stump" Andrew Goldfarb** - Goldfarb's acclaimed comic series. A magical and weird journey into the horrors of everyday life. **164 pages $11**

BB-099 **"Pickled Apocalypse of Pancake Island" Cameron Pierce** A demented fairy tale about a pickle, a pancake, and the apocalypse. **102 pages $8**

BB-100 **"Slag Attack" Andersen Prunty** - Slag Attack features four visceral, noir stories about the living, crawling apocalypse. A slag is what survivors are calling the slug-like maggots raining from the sky, burrowing inside people, and hollowing out their flesh and their sanity. **148 pages $11**

BB-101 **"Slaughterhouse High" Robert Devereaux** - A place where schools are built with secret passageways, rebellious teens get zippers installed in their mouths and genitals, and once a year, on that special night, one couple is slaughtered and the bits of their bodies are kept as souvenirs. **304 pages $13**

BB-102 **"The Emerald Burrito of Oz" John Skipp & Marc Levinthal** OZ IS REAL! Magic is real! The gate is really in Kansas! And America is finally allowing Earth tourists to visit this weird-ass, mysterious land. But when Gene of Los Angeles heads off for summer vacation in the Emerald City, little does he know that a war is brewing...a war that could destroy both worlds. **280 pages $13**

BB-103 **"The Vegan Revolution... with Zombies" David Agranoff** When there's no more meat in hell, the vegans will walk the earth. **160 pages $11**

BB-104 **"The Flappy Parts" Kevin L Donihe** - Poems about bunnies, LSD, and police abuse. You know, things that matter. 132 **pages $11**

BB-105 **"Sorry I Ruined Your Orgy" Bradley Sands** - Bizarro humorist Bradley Sands returns with one of the strangest, most hilarious collections of the year. **130 pages $11**

BB-106 **"Mr. Magic Realism" Bruce Taylor** - Like Golden Age science fiction comics written by Freud, *Mr. Magic Realism* is a strange, insightful adventure that spans the furthest reaches of the galaxy, exploring the hidden caverns in the hearts and minds of men, women, aliens, and biomechanical cats. **152 pages $11**

BB-107 **"Zombies and Shit" Carlton Mellick III** - "Battle Royale" meets "Return of the Living Dead." Mellick's bizarro tribute to the zombie genre. **308 pages $13**

BB-108 **"The Cannibal's Guide to Ethical Living" Mykle Hansen** - Over a five star French meal of fine wine, organic vegetables and human flesh, a lunatic delivers a witty, chilling, disturbingly sane argument in favor of eating the rich.. **184 pages $11**

BB-109 **"Starfish Girl" Athena Villaverde** - In a post-apocalyptic underwater dome society, a girl with a starfish growing from her head and an assassin with sea anenome hair are on the run from a gang of mutant fish men. **160 pages $11**

BB-110 **"Lick Your Neighbor" Chris Genoa** - Mutant ninjas, a talking whale, kung fu masters, maniacal pilgrims, and an alcoholic clown populate Chris Genoa's surreal, darkly comical and unnerving reimagining of the first Thanksgiving. **303 pages $13**

BB-111 **"Night of the Assholes" Kevin L. Donihe** - A plague of assholes is infecting the countryside. Normal everyday people are transforming into jerks, snobs, dicks, and douchebags. And they all have only one purpose: to make your life a living hell.. **192 pages $11**

BB-112 **"Jimmy Plush, Teddy Bear Detective" Garrett Cook** - Hardboiled cases of a private detective trapped within a teddy bear body. **180 pages $11**